SPIES IN CANAAN

SPIES IN CANAAN

David Park

BLOOMSBURY PUBLISHING
LONDON · OXFORD · NEW YORK · NEW DELHI · SYDNEY

BLOOMSBURY PUBLISHING
Bloomsbury Publishing Plc
50 Bedford Square, London, WC1B 3DP, UK
29 Earlsfort Terrace, Dublin 2, Ireland

BLOOMSBURY, BLOOMSBURY PUBLISHING and the Diana logo
are trademarks of Bloomsbury Publishing Plc

First published in Great Britain 2022

A catalogue record for this book is available from the British Library

ISBN: HB: 978-1-5266-3193-0; TPB: 978-1-5266-3196-1;
EBOOK: 978-1-5266-3195-4; EPDF: 978-1-5266-5571-4

2 4 6 8 10 9 7 5 3 1

Typeset by Integra Software Services Pvt. Ltd.
Printed and bound in Great Britain by CPI Group (UK) Ltd, Croydon CR0 4YY

To find out more about our authors and books visit www.bloomsbury.com
and sign up for our newsletters

For Alberta, who is the very best of us

GHOST SOLDIERS

My cup is full and running over. A book full and running over with stories. So many stories you could never remember every one and all of them are true because God has told the storytellers what words to use. A giant killed by a single slingshot, walls that come tumbling down, men who walk through fire and are not consumed. Where there is no death except for the deserving because in the early-morning light the stone is rolled away and they tell me that is why I never have to die if I believe with all my heart. And so I sit on the Sunday-school pew with swinging legs, try to believe as I sing,

> Twelve spies went to spy in Canaan
> Ten were bad, two were good
> Some saw the giants big and tall
> Some saw the grapes in clusters fall
> Some saw that God was in it all
> Ten were bad, two were good.

and I do the falling-grapes-and-clusters motion with my hands, flex the muscles I don't have to represent the giants and hold up the right number of fingers for the good and bad spies. Then when it's time, I give my collection coins that are to be split equally between the orphans and the lepers. And the silver-haired Miss Reynolds brings out the flannelgraph, sticks pictures on it about a boy who lives in a barrel, but I don't like this story so much as some of the others because I like to think the pictures for myself. So I see the little boy who brings five barley loaves and two small fishes and how they feed the five thousand and sometimes when I open my brown paper lunch bag in school I know how hard it must be to do a miracle. But there are miracles everywhere in these stories – a child born in old age, a withered hand healed, a storm told to be still. So many miracles I can hardly remember them all.

But there is one miracle that as a child frightens me and sometimes creeps inside my dreams, and only years later I see that it's not a miracle after all. After the plagues, after the pestilence, an angel with black beating wings, knife in hand, swooping in at midnight across the silent desert sands to kill the firstborn, killing Pharaoh's child and even that of the captive in the dungeon. Killing the unbelievers. I am a firstborn and in my dreams I hear their screams rent the night. In later life it flares back again in all its raw intensity when I watch the pictures of Isis ravaging across desert sands. But as a child I believe that if my father has painted blood on the doorposts and lintels we will be safe, all those who have followed this command will be unharmed, and so I lie perfectly still, imagine the door to our world painted with blood and, amidst the silence that enfolds the sleeping house, strain to hear the angel's wings passing in the darkness.

I walk out to the garden and into the late-afternoon air, needing a little time to think, and look at the magnolia. It's identical to the one we had in our London residence. Julia had planted this new one the very year we moved into the house, a house that was to be our permanent abode and our very last home. And for her it was, its finality unanticipated when cancer granted her the shortest of leases. There is still a lingering languid perfume from the creamy white flowers, even though the fierce flush of its earlier blossom has slowly faded with no trace of Lowell's 'murderous five days' white' igniting the coming evening, and when I touch the blossom it feels fleshy, ready to break in my hands, the soft pulp seared with a delicate blush of pink.

I take the petals, go back inside and set them in front of her photograph then return to my desk. Hannah, my housekeeper, comes to the doorway to tell me she's going and that's she left me something light for my supper in the kitchen. I have a growing dread of these moments. As always she asks, 'Will that be all?' and as always I answer yes and thank her but have no way to tell her that after she goes the house will fall again into a silence and increasingly a part of me wants her to never leave. I listen to the front door close, hear the familiar complaint of her car's elderly engine as it starts up and try to focus again on the words.

But I'm distracted once more by the padded envelope on my desk that contains a DVD and the briefest of notes from someone I knew over forty years ago. Someone with whom I shared a part of my life in a far-off world that was short in duration but whose memories continue to accompany the counting down of my years. And there's something in me doesn't want to view it, because I don't always trust the past and sometimes, if you stumble into it unaware, it can pull you in like quicksand, drag you down until you go under. And I know I have to hold my head up, so for the moment at least I set the envelope to one side and try to find my own path back, exercise some control over what is rising to meet me.

But perhaps I'm only avoiding committing to the details because it goes against the grain, against all the values of discretion that years of service inculcated. Discretion, secrecy, silence – these are still the trade's accepted virtues, even in an age of supposed freedom of information where the idealists believe that it never requires a price to be paid. Those we bring through rendition to sit in cells with their interrogators in places that don't exist and those we subject to 'enhanced techniques' know a different truth – that knowledge is often the most dangerous thing of all to possess and that in this world the safest lives are those who know nothing. But only if you are believed. Yes, only if you are believed.

How to tell the story and be granted this belief, even if never as completely as I would wish? So much distance has been travelled from those far-off days and there are other things fixed firmly inside the codes of confidentiality I once worked by, and perhaps, above all, the redactions we all make on the pages of our past. And yes, when you alone carry the information, it is, of course, a pressing and constant temptation to omit or even reshape the moments when we were less than we wanted to be, or make ourselves the victim rather than the perpetrator of our own lives. I've realised that already.

Perhaps to counter that I have a little postcard of one of Rembrandt's self-portraits above my desk. I glance at it often, think how tempting it must have been to leave the world a noble image, one infused with an enduring grandeur. But this is not what I see. Instead he gives us the face of an old man saddened and wearied by the incomprehensible flurries of life that have carried him here. His clothes are black, his eyes look away from the darkness that occupies one side of the canvas, but it's as if it's slowly moving towards his face and already seeping into his skin. A silent dignity survives the centuries. Perhaps such a final dignity will always be out of my reach because I think the only way to attain it is by telling all of the truth and I'm not sure if I can do that, or even if all of the truth is something that can ever fully exist any more in this world where the Chinese whispers of the Internet era have resulted in what we blithely call fake news.

My story isn't inspired by an awareness of the dying of the light. I'm no longer young, of course, but in that brief hinterland that exists just before you become very old. My health is generally good, only the arthritis in my left knee that sadly prevents too much tennis a nagging nod to mortality. So I hope there are plenty of miles to go before I sleep. Nor is it about rage, because I'm not fired by an intensity of anger but rather mostly just regret and the longings you think should have withered on the vine with advancing age. That's one of the strangest things about getting old – you assume that all the restlessness and confusions of your younger years should, with the fullness of time, be replaced by an inner security, a solidity that preserves from the high tides of life, when actually what endures is just a different current of troubling uncertainties. And if it doesn't flow with the same spring fuse of youth and you think yourself cosseted by whatever money and status you've accrued, you can never swear that a single moment, whether in a waitress's fleeting smile or a juddering memory, might not see those same defences permanently eroded.

I was a small-town prairie boy whose featureless, unbroken horizons were filled only with what could be conjured from dreams and, as I grew up, the endless supply of books I borrowed from our local library, where trespassing dust trembled nervously in the thin shafts of light slanting through the windows' wooden slats as if wary of discovery. And it was in this same library that I first imagined I was in love, in love with Mrs Hartford, one of the two librarians and mother of two boys who attended the same school as I did. I'd watch her through the stacks, surreptitiously part the spines of books to allow my view, secretly track the course of her work routines by listening for the press of her black patent shoes against the wooden floorboards, but if she so much as smiled at someone she probably thought of as a serious boy and keen reader, I'd blush and lower my head to whatever text I was studying, momentarily mortified by the thought that she could read my adoration as plainly as the words on a page. I would always wait to ensure that she was at the front desk and the one to stamp my books and, as she did it, I'd feast on the piled and pinned glory of her hair, the delicacy of her fingers, the whiteness of the underside of her wrist. Hoped one day she might come to work with the pins removed from her hair so it fell in auburn drifts about her shoulders. Hoped she'd be impressed by my reading choices. Perhaps those months of painful infatuation were the genesis of my sense that love and books are somehow sensually indivisible, that one can't fully exist without the other.

What little of the world that existed outside my library-book pages had been pared even more by an evangelical Presbyterian upbringing and decent but plain-living parents. My father, who had an agricultural seed business, was an elder in our local red-brick church, superintendent of its Sunday school, and his sea of faith never ebbed throughout the rest of his life, until that life was stolen by something else. A faith symbolised by a burning bush, but what smouldered unquenched through my late teenage years was a desire for something and somewhere to which I couldn't even give a name, much less understand how it might be attained, until gradually those stories with which I had grown up came to be overlaid with different ones. So Jonah and his whale was replaced by an old man struggling to land a giant fish – an old man who in his youth from the deck of his boat had seen lions walking on an African beach – and the feeding of the five thousand was pushed aside by what felt like the even greater miracle of Rose of Sharon suckling a dying man. And these stories gave me a different world in which to live, told me I wasn't crazy and more than anything that I wasn't alone, while whispering that the seemingly endless stretch to the horizon might in time come to be filled with something I hoped would reveal itself to be love.

But Saigon had no horizon, no empty spaces that hadn't already been claimed and filled full of unmediated life. The city flared intensely against the senses the way its incessant traffic flowed all around you, and whatever nervous resistance I might have initially offered was soon swept away in absolute bewildered surrender. In those first few days after my arrival it wasn't languid oriental images, or a Zen-like calm, that pressed against my consciousness but rather the frenetic intensity of the moment from which there was no escape and from which I desired none. So on those early mornings when I walked the couple of blocks to the downtown offices where I worked I was almost overwhelmed by the scenes and sensations that blazed through me.

Men brushing the streets with what looked like fantails of twigs, swishing rotting crimson and yellow fruit into the gutter; already a stream of Hondas weaving round cyclos and cyclists, one with a gas cylinder propped on the handlebars, one with hens in a bamboo cage and a pyramid of boxes so the rider was barely visible; an open-fronted barber's shop with a poster of James Dean in the doorway and the bee-like buzz of clippers zipping; the sound of the Mamas and the Papas from an open window and paper lanterns hanging from a wooden rail; the spicy sizzle of a noodle stall; the wavering blue wick of a welding flame in a courtyard as a man worked on a bike repair; sunlight splaying against beer and soft-drinks kiosks and under one of the scantily leafed tamarind trees that lined each side of the street a trio of shoeshine boys called out to me, their voices high like a harmonised descant. They weren't the only inhabitants of the city who spoke to me those mornings. There was a begging, legless vet on a bamboo mat always in the same spot who held out his wooden bowl; an old woman all in black perched on a little stool massaging her feet who raised her face to me and uttered what might have been a daily greeting or a curse; and a young woman with sleep in her eyes wearing a white halter top and denim hot pants, who invited me inside the darkened doorway of the steam and massage parlour behind her.

My very first night in that city, however, had seen me make a fool of myself. A combination of jet lag, some questionable airline food and a general sense of disorientation saw me slip into a fractured sleep, awash with the swirl of crazed images that had their origin in television's portrayal of the war. I woke repeatedly before forcing myself into a shallow doze but suddenly jerked awake as gun and heavy-arms fire burst all around the building. My first night in Saigon and I was taking incoming fire. I tumbled out of bed, ducked to the window and tried to look out without making a target of myself. Intermittent, luridly-coloured light flared behind a building on the other side of the road. I backtracked and opened the door, then stepped into the corridor to meet an American who appeared to be responding to the attack by taking a six-pack of beer and a girly magazine to his room, three doors down from mine.

'Fireworks waken you?' he asked as he shuffled the beer and magazine to allow himself to turn his key in the lock. 'Any excuse and they're letting off firecrackers like it's the Fourth of July.'

I nodded and then as nonchalantly as I could rubbed some imaginary sleep out of my eyes, simulated a yawn and returned to my room.

It was the closest I ever came to being under fire. I worked in a white-stuccoed, red-tiled, three-storeyed former French administration office guarded at its entrance by a couple of Nung guards who lounged against the metal gates but never let their M16s leave their hands and who on that first morning, when I ostentatiously showed them my pass, looked at me, not with my hoped-for respect, but the same disdain that every soldier has for REMFs — rear-echelon motherfuckers. And that's the thing about the war because when we were still in the shadow of the

Paris Peace Accords finally being signed, which we know now only served to briefly postpone the inevitable, it felt initially at least like some distant sideshow from which I was physically and even morally disconnected, even though I was there because of it. Having been recruited and trained a short while earlier, my role was essentially to shuffle paper, sort the torrent of intelligence reports that streamed in from various sources, transcribe, collate, summarise, cross-reference, highlight things that required urgent responses and occasionally use my knowledge of French when needed. We had sources inside the French Embassy in Saigon and in Paris filing on a regular basis. I was little more than a clerk with security clearance. My ID card simply said I was an employee of the American Embassy.

We look at what happens to us through the prism of our own inherent stumbling day-to-day lives and not through the printed page and the long lens of history. So my memory of those years isn't dominated by the bloody images that we've all seen on our television screens, or the names on the Wall, even though I'm eternally conscious of them and deeply respectful of the human suffering repre-sented by everyone who died on all sides in that distant land. The past is shaped instead by something intensely and chaotically personal, so sometimes it feels as if it's part of a puzzle that doesn't fit into the overall and ordered composition established by that well-documented history. It's history, of course, whose judgement pronounces us guilty of terrible things and I accept that verdict, share my culpability. But the young man walking to his office on those Saigon mornings, and who had arrived belatedly in the final years leading up to the war's sudden and dramatic end, believed he wasn't there to kill people or drop napalm. Wasn't really there to do anyone any harm, and whatever personal revisionism my subsequent experiences and the passing of the years have brought to that belief, it had not then sown seed much less taken root. Mostly I just sat on the building's second floor with the louvred windows half-closed in a futile attempt to keep out some of the city's broiling heat, read about what other people were doing in so-called intelligence reports from our army of agents but which often seemed merely attempts to justify their continued existence on Uncle Sam's payroll, and occasionally translated documents or tapes. There was no proper air conditioning and the wooden blades of the electric ceiling fans did little to relieve our discomfort, so their main purpose seemed to be to gently levitate the pile of papers with which my desk was usually covered.

My college professor was the person who recruited me, doubtless deciding that any sober young man who permanently wore a jacket to lectures complete with leather elbow patches, handed in high-quality assignments on time and appeared to have few friends or social distractions, had to have the Stars and Stripes tattooed on his heart. His respected and flattering opinion – and mostly in my life I believe I have been a person compliant with what I thought of as higher authority – combined with the absence of an alternative salary-earning career meant I went along with it. There were times during the period of training when my assessors didn't share his confidence and, after one of their many psychological profiles revealed my moral ambiguity about actually having to kill someone, they took their foot off the gas and designated me as a desk jockey with the same sort of disdain that I saw in the Nung guards' eyes.

By the time I got posted to Saigon, most other Americans had gone home. Nixon's process of Vietnamising the war had seen the removal of ground troops, collapsing a sizeable proportion of the rampant economy that had blossomed to indulge their every need. Now, mostly, the bars and hotels were frequented by private contractors, the engineers and specialists needed to service the remaining mechanics of conflict and the still-burgeoning army of bureaucrats and intelligence people who were supposed to bring the conflict, if not to victory, then to a satisfactory face-saving conclusion. It would be easy and better to say I never believed in the war but a naive part of me, initially at least, bought into that traditional view that we were building a wall against something that otherwise was going to keep on rolling until it reached our own shore – was intending to flatten our world with the same intensity of a tornado I once experienced as a child. So I was to be a small part of stopping that invasion. I guess too I had been stirred by JFK's words: 'Let every nation know, whether it wishes us well or ill, that we shall pay any price, bear any burden, meet any hardship, support any friend, oppose any foe, in order to assure the survival and success of liberty.'

The idealism of these words had been gradually eroded when the reality of the price needing to be paid rendered itself inescapably visible with every flag-draped coffin shouldered across airport runways. And after the revelations about the My Lai massacre it was difficult to persist with any genuinely unsullied sense of moral imperative, so some things had to be compartmentalised and held at a distance from personal conscience, however dishonest and indeed culpable this sounds. It's what happens when your nation goes to war and you serve part of it, even if your status is never much higher than all the other grunts and your hand never actually fires a weapon. But it was still a shock to hear Calley's attempted defence that he was following orders, even if it was the only one I guess open to him, seemingly oblivious to the terrible historical resonance of those words.

The idea of building a protective wall, however, is still the basis of our foreign-policy thinking as I've always known and seen it practised. Hawks and doves, isolationists and interventionists, neo this and neo that – whatever way you want to see it, whatever names you use – but what it all boils down to is that sometimes we pay and equip others to act on our behalf in an attempt to stem that flow – people who generally prove unreliable and prone to fragmentation and internecine conflict. People who are either irredeemably corrupt or who eventually come back and bite our ass, usually with the very means with which we enthusiastically supplied them. We naively persist too in the belief that superior technology allows us to bend the world to our will as we assume the role of Jupiter, hurl our lightning bolts down from the sky, whether it's LBJ's Rolling Thunder or George W. Bush's Shock and Awe. At other times, despite proclaiming we've learned the lessons of Vietnam, we put our own feet on the ground, take the hits and then when the heat turns itself up, retire, pretending we've left something solid behind us when the reality is it'll be toppled by the first strong wind that blows. And even though we now increasingly use drones and technology, our own ghost soldiers, to replace the human, not even 9/11 and our supposed global war on terror has changed the way we think about the world beyond our shores in any meaningful way. Sometimes I think I did pretty well spinning two books out of these meagre realities.

But such philosophical musings were far from my mind on that first day when fresh-faced, and yes, despite the heat, wearing the same jacket with its slightly frayed cuffs I had worn in college, I nervously climbed the stairs with their flaking paint on the walls and air of colonial decay, then was escorted into a large open room with perhaps twenty men and women working at desks and in one corner a stuttering teletype machine. I had been dispatched to take the desk and various duties of Nils Nordstrom who had been sent home suffering from an exotic strain of hepatitis and whose left-behind detritus I touched with an initial reluctance, in the mistaken belief that I might somehow contract whatever virus had laid him low. The head of the department was a tall, bald-headed austere man with rimless spectacles, wearing a stone-coloured safari suit, who, after ushering me into an office lined with filing cabinets and metal shelving but elegantly softened by white orchids and books, talked me through everything, pausing at intervals to inspect me by looking over the top of his reading glasses. He was called Nathaniel Greenberg, a Francophile who probably secretly lamented Dien Bien Phu had ever happened, and despite, as I later found out, coming from the Brick City of Newark, always conveyed the impression that his reed-like frame could be blown over by a strong breeze. On his desk was a copy of Flaubert's *L'Éducation sentimentale* – he'd obviously read up on my background – and, when he asked if I knew it, was clearly pleased that I did. I also learned later that it was his chosen means of evaluating any new recruit with responsibility for translation. And now I think that reading nineteenth-century French novels was what he mostly did during his working day.

'So what you have to remember, Michael,' he said after outlining procedures and protocols, 'is that everything we do here is of the utmost importance. And that's why the closest attention must be paid to detail. Take nothing for granted and know that a single word might carry more significance than you could ever imagine. Lives might depend on it. Many, many lives.'

He nodded at the pleasing solemnity of what he had just uttered, and made a little bridge of his fingers, and because of his height it felt as if I was a boy being addressed by my high-school principal. When he went on speaking I registered more clearly the breathlessness that underlaid his speech, so that it was as if his words were afloat on a current of air that at any moment might expire.

'And of course I don't need to tell you that everything you see is classified and carries a high security rating. And nothing, but nothing, goes in and out of this building without my knowledge and approval,' he added, his hollow cheeks tightening with effort and a light stipple of sweat beading his brow.

By the end of the first month I pondered how the supposed high level of security he spoke of allowed a daily delivery of lunchtime meals from various vendors, the frequent appearance of young women from a nearby flower kiosk who flirted with the guards, a rota of cleaning maids who moved through the building like silent ghosts at irregular times of the day and never looked anyone in the eye, as if being noticed would challenge the reality of their existence, and of course the constant arrival of couriers. I never quite got used either to seeing lizards scurrying across walls or suddenly appearing from under cabinets.

We were never a large sophisticated operation like the one they had run in the Combined Intelligence Centre out at Tan Son Nhut, with their microfilm databases and automatic data processing systems. Although I never fully discovered how our role related to a wider context, it struck me that we were a quiet, low-tech offshoot that existed at the discreet behest of certain interests. Despite at times feeling like a cottage industry, there was a steady stream of work landing on my desk – telexes and tapes of what I assumed were prisoner or defector interviews; written reports from various agents in the field who had probably done the same job for the French; updates from our sources inside Thieu's administration which mostly outlined in sometimes lurid detail the latest machinations and corruptions of high-ranking officials. Machiavellian plots from Cambodia on supposed attempts by the French to restore Sihanouk and generally mischief-make. There was, too, an ongoing investigation into the existence of 'ghost soldiers' – a lucrative scam where military commanders added names of non-existent soldiers to their lists and creamed off their wages. In addition there were endless reports continuing to arrive from Paris, where a range of supposed insiders filed on everything: from the daily facial expressions of the North Vietnamese, to what groceries were delivered to their places of residence. Often it came to feel that, just as a daily newspaper needed to fill its columns, so these sources needed to justify their existence by the number of words on the page.

Each of the tapes or written documents bore a code and a log number that designated its classification and who it was intended for. When I had completed any form of translation work I was obliged to take the finished transcripts into Greenberg's office and he would wordlessly gesture me to sit while he pretended to peruse them, never responding in any way to what was in them but keen rather to explore nuances of language and I supposed to display his greater knowledge. It felt like getting my homework marked and in fact he did always have a red pen in his hand. Whether it was because my work passed muster or whether it was because he approved of me, or rather my pleasure in literature, I don't know, but whichever, the red pen seemed more of a prop than a necessity. On one such engagement at the end of my first week he asked me my favourite French novel and when I told him it was *Le Grand Meaulnes* he put his pen down and, with that slightly breathless voice that sometimes made it sound as if speech wearied him, said, 'Ah Michael, the innocence of youth.' He was smiling at me and I didn't know if he found my choice foolish. But he said nothing further and, as he dismissed me, began to sort the papers I had given him into the hard-backed files that sat on the shelves behind him and which were distinguishable from each other only by the codes on their spines.

During those first few weeks I was mentored by the two Vietnamese who occupied the desks closest to mine. Probably in their mid-twenties, they – in my eyes at least – just looked like work colleagues. But they were a couple in the full sense of the word, although I didn't realise this at first until one night I saw them strolling hand in hand along Nguyen Hue Boulevard. She called herself Corrine in what I guessed was a conscious decision to Westernise her identity and he was called Danh – it was only the first time I saw his name written down that I understood he hadn't done the same. They smiled a lot and at intervals shared green tea with me from the large flasks they kept under their desks. Sometimes at lunch they would invite me to sit with them in the garden at the back of the building. There were some rattan chairs and plastic tables and someone had strung an awning from a couple of the mostly leafless trees so that it was possible to find refuge from the sun. Softening the back wall's coping of barbed wire were jasmine and hibiscus plants from where cicadas accompanied our conversation. At my insistence they taught me enough Vietnamese to master the basic courtesies.

'Where do you live in America?' Danh enquired that first day but, when I told him, I knew it was a geographical blank.

'You find things strange here?' he asked and then seemed pleased when I said that I didn't, that I liked it. That I liked everything.

They ventured other questions politely about America and my college courses. They were curious too about simple things such as whether I had a car and other countries I had travelled to. Then, when they saw that I was open to their questions, Corrine tentatively asked me the one with which I would come increasingly familiar until it reached a point, further down the line, when I read it in the eyes of every Vietnamese I encountered.

'Will you stay?' she asked before turning her gaze away, as if worried that she had been too forward, and I knew that she wasn't really referring to me but rather was asking about my nation's future intentions and, a little flattered by the supposed knowledge the question bestowed on me, I paused before replying.

'We're here to fulfil our commitments to the Vietnamese people. We will stand shoulder to shoulder with you for as long as we're needed,' I said, pleased by my heartfelt sincerity and probably a little regretful that I couldn't deliver it with the same gravel-throated gravitas of a Kissinger, hopelessly unaware that my priggish naivety did little to reassure them when every day they read of Congress's increased resistance to funding increased military aid and the intensity of the opposition to the war sweeping across my homeland.

'They say top people's wives and all their belongings are being flown out,' Danh said, smiling a little to hide his obvious embarrassment.

'I don't know anything about it,' I answered truthfully, worried that more such questions would expose the obvious fact that I didn't know very much about anything but, as a codicil, added, 'We're here to the end. Never doubt that.'

How easy it is to lie when you want the lie to be true. They simply nodded in reply and Corrine poured me more green tea for which I expressed my genuine gratitude while wishing it was the swirl of a black coffee. Overhead a large butterfly landed on the top of the awning, its silhouette momentarily deprived of its intense colours. Two other of my male Vietnamese colleagues played a languid game of badminton where the aim seemed to be to hit the shuttle-cock as high in the air as possible then dreamily watch its fall to earth. Danh gently raised his finger to the awning where the butterfly was resting and watched it flurry reluctantly into flight.

The days were getting hotter and I had finally abandoned my jacket, replacing it with open-necked short-sleeved white shirts and black pants that I felt might pass muster if anyone decided to inspect me. But it was already evident that no one higher up in my organisation was particularly interested in me. In one of our daily encounters Greenberg had made a perfunctory but polite enquiry as to whether I was settling in and rolled his eyes when I told him where I was billeted. Where he himself lived was a mystery but there were rumours he enjoyed a rather tasteful villa complete with cook, maid and a coterie of cats that appeared to be his favoured out-of-work companions.

I was housed in a small and unattractive three-floor apartment block for unmarried officers not far from Lam Son Square that was overseen – and I'm not sure if her role was official or self-appointed – by an elderly Vietnamese woman called Madame Binh who inhabited a first-floor apartment but seemed to have extended her residency to include the foyer and often when I entered or left she was sitting in a cane chair with a cat on her lap. She was more than just a kind of *soi-disant* concierge but someone who also nosed into all our business and rooms like the owner of a boarding house determined to ensure the propriety of her establishment. She moved as noiselessly as her cat and she might appear at any time in any part of the block, ostensibly on some errand that was supposedly in your interest or to impart some piece of news or gossip of a usually imaginary importance.

It was there that I met Corley Rodgers for the first time. I had left the door open in the vain hope that it might make the room seem bigger than it actually was as I tried to rearrange its meagre contents, when there was a light knock and I turned to see him standing there.

'So you drew the short straw too,' he said, brushing away the lock of blond hair that persisted in falling towards his eyes as he spoke.

'The short straw?'

'Yes, getting holed-up in this dump. No offence but you must be as far down the pecking order as me. If either of us were considered even half-important we'd be swanking it up over at the Duc until they found us something better than this.'

'The Duc?'

'The Duc Hotel, where you live in decent style. It's the penthouse suite and this is a flophouse – the plumbing is ancient and always wants to let you down when you need it most.' He walked in uninvited and looked at the view from the window. 'The Duc has a good restaurant with Home Sweet Home food, a swimming pool with new sun deck, a cinema and just about anything else you might need to forget that you're here.'

He dropped the flimsy curtain dismissively, as if the view had been as dismal as he'd expected, then turned and offered his hand. After our introductions we both struggled for something to fill the silence.

'How long have you been here?' I asked.

'Two years. You fresh out of training?'

I hesitated. It didn't seem like a good start to my career to announce that fact to a complete stranger but he smiled, that boyish smile which together with the colour of his hair made him look like someone about to go surfing or cheer his team from sun-kissed bleachers, before he said, 'We're all Langley boys here but getting allocated to Madame Binh's means you're a water-carrier, a grunt in Uncle Sam's secret army.'

There was something reassuring, an artless openness about him, that invited disclosure and like a new boy just arrived in school I needed to make friends who could show me the ropes. But I was nervous, too, in a David Copperfield–Steerforth way and half-expecting that he might suggest minding my spending money for me.

'I work a desk,' I told him.

'You speak the lingo?'

'No. Mostly I just move paper and some French translation when it's needed.'

'So you're a REMF then,' he said, still smiling, 'not a highly trained killer about to go solo into the jungle?'

'Afraid not. Just words on a page. Shuffling papers, sometimes writing transcripts. And you?'

'I do words on a page too, so we have that in common. I tell stories. I've worked for USIA and CORD.' When he saw that the names were just more of those endless acronyms with which the war effort was littered, he explained they stood for the United States Information Agency and Civil Operations and Rural Development Support.

'You tell stories?'

'Yes, I write upbeat stories about how many wonderful things we're doing here,' he said, then flopped on the bed, making its springs creak. 'Propaganda really, if truth be told. Then I try to get them placed in the press back home.'

'What sort of stories?'

He propped his head on the pillow of his arms and stared at the ceiling before answering, 'How we come bearing gifts to the needy. How we build roads and schools. Bring sanitation and clean water. Bring candy and toothbrushes. Bring Uncle Sam kindness.' Then, blowing a stream of air up through his fringe, added, 'You need to get an electric fan for in here. You can use your PX card, pick one up at the warehouse. I can go with you if you like.'

As I saw him looking at my meagre collection of clothes hanging in the narrow wardrobe which had no door, it felt as if he was inspecting them, so in an attempt to distract him I asked where he was based.

'The Lincoln Library mostly but I get around. Listen, I know a really good tailor's just behind Tu Do Street – he'll run you up everything you need for very little.'

And then, as he lay stretched out on my bed, he slipped into full Steerforth mode, with advice on the best restaurants, how if I wanted we could go bowling at the airbase, swim at Le Cercle Sportif, even some weekend perhaps head down to Vung Tau, a beach resort two hours' drive from Saigon. I was cautious in my responses, not wishing to appear stand-offish but not wanting to commit myself to a relationship when I knew almost nothing about him. So we lapsed into a silence that I tried to pretend was merely caused by my preoccupation with trying to get my room shipshape. But then as he saw the dozen or so novels that added the ballast to my life and which I had arranged on a makeshift shelf, he became suddenly animated, springing off the bed and lifting them. A couple were dropped dismissively but he held on to others as if his hands held the Holy Grail.

'You read?' he asked, as if it was the most unlikely of discoveries. 'I've never met anyone here yet who read anything other than porn mags, sci-fi or hard-boiled detective crap. But what's with so much Steinbeck?'

I could have told him that discovering Steinbeck at the age of sixteen was one of those formative moments that helped me understand there really existed a life which couldn't be explained by the beliefs that had been given to me. About reading the end of *The Grapes of Wrath* where Rose of Sharon suckles the dying man and feeling profoundly changed in ways I couldn't even begin to explain. But instead I simply said, 'I like him.'

'For sure,' he said, 'but Fitzgerald's my main man – all those blue lawns and green lights. Filling your head with dreams.'

'"Boats against the current … "'

'"Borne back ceaselessly into the past … "'

We both smiled, and suddenly we were members of the same club, naively costumed in our brightly coloured uniforms of a shared romantic readiness. And it was that smug unspoken belief that we were somehow intellectuals that inured us in part against some of the ridicule and indignities that we encountered in our menial roles.

'Hemingway too, of course,' he said. 'He'd have turned up here following the action. Do you know what he said about writing?' And when I told him I didn't he straightened in a mock-heroic way and declaimed, '"There is nothing to writing. All you do is sit down at a typewriter and bleed."'

Later in a pavement café, over a couple of Tiger Beers that tasted so bitter I resolved to avoid them at all costs in the future, he revealed a little self-consciously that he was doing his own bleeding and writing a novel about the war. But it was proving so difficult that sometimes he occasionally was driven to taking a notebook to the bar at the Continental Hotel where Graham Greene had supposedly worked on *The Quiet American*, as if in the hope that some psychic transference of inspiration might take place. Even though I hadn't asked, he told me he couldn't let me see it yet as it was in its early stages and he was still trying to get things shaped in his head. I never did get to see it and never knew whether it existed in any tangible way or was merely the product of his imaginative desire, but as we sat in the sultry, slowly ebbing heat of the night, where the city's inexhaustible variety of life coursed around us, I was prepared to believe that all things were possible.

And he did go with me on my first trip to the PX Exchange – we went to one in the Cholon district for reasons I can't remember. It was an Aladdin's cave packed to the gills with everything under the sun. I'd never seen anything quite like it. And it wasn't just basics like toiletries, but clothes, stereos, guitars, watches, refrigerators, cameras, all type of booze and every home comfort that might be physically and psychologically needed to survive in a foreign land. And, unless I've imagined it, they had machines for making popcorn and ice cream. While I bought an electric fan, Corley studied a display of engagement rings but didn't buy anything other than a carton of Hershey Bars and some pants that looked like they belonged on a golf course.

As time passed, the reports piling up on my desk increasingly pointed to the undisguised impermanence of the peace, with constant accounts of breaches of the cease-fire and warnings about troop and supply movements, the build-up of military strength in a range of key areas. But still at this time just words on a page. There were, too, a great many about the jostling for position inside Thieu's administration and military command, with a frequent bitter belief that they had been sold out in Paris. The tone seemed ever shriller, less likely to offer fence-sitting ambiguity in their analyses, and I passed them on to whoever's job it was to make some deeper sense of them. And when I finished each day I mostly forgot about their contents and tried to fit into the life that had been given to me and, with the passing of the months, liked to believe I had assumed the confident manner of someone who belonged.

This, initially at least, was my protected and singular world. I bought fruit in the central market and outside the Botanical Gardens; played tennis or sat poolside at Le Cercle Sportif sipping *citron pressé* with Corley, thinking ourselves suddenly inducted into sophistication and trying not to stare at the young women in their bikinis, or those draped on the arms of older men of various nationalities and mysterious backgrounds; drank coffees in Tu Do Street; had a better quality of beer on the roof terrace of the Caravelle Hotel, or on the veranda of the Continental Palace, with its green shutters and slightly shabby interiors and where it always felt as if the waiters in their white uniforms were privy to secrets from days gone by. Mostly Corley would chaperone me round these locations and talk about how his novel was progressing. I soon realised, as he played the role of mentor, that he welcomed my friendship because he didn't seem to have any other close friends, and a couple of times after I had turned him down because I was having a meal with Corrine and Danh, or meeting up with other work colleagues, I detected a sense of hurt, as if they had replaced him. Once, too, when we were at the Rex Hotel, a group of journalists mostly the worse for drink shouted derisively at him and mockingly called on him to share some good news with them. We pretended not to hear.

So time went on, and as I lay on my bed some nights before sleep I thought of the prairie town where I had grown up and where my parents and my younger sister still lived. A world that somehow managed to be expansive and open in its physical parameters but constraining in its effects, and I felt a certain smugness that I could evaluate it so clearly and had escaped its confines. I was already stepping out on a wider stage, had access to vistas and experiences that my hometown's inhabitants could never imagine, and I knew whatever happened I could never return in any permanent way. And yet I still enjoyed the simple letters that arrived regularly from home, with their expressions of affection, the litany of small-town news – births, deaths, marriages, and the inevitable reporting of barely changing weather. I had been deliberately vague about my work, perhaps enjoying bestowing on it a greater sense of mystery than it deserved – until, feeling guilty about their increasing expressions of concern for my safety, I wrote explaining that I was safely ensconced in an administrative job, maintaining a little hint of my self-importance by saying I couldn't elaborate due to reasons of national security.

But there is also something else I need to explain, and I don't know if it will be easily grasped or not, but it's an important aspect of this part of the story and should be told, even though it may only be understood by those whose origins are similar to mine. In a significant part, I grew up on the pews of a church that believed in individual salvation and, despite the wave of social change and summers of love, large swathes of my fellow countrymen and women remained immune to the Age of Aquarius, registering only bewilderment and clinging to the age-old beliefs that had appeared to nurture the nation and preserve its soul. By the end of my teens I was no longer a traditional believer but something to which I can't give a name stopped me embracing the new world on offer even though it wasn't exactly rushing towards me with open arms. I had been taught that I was in the world but not of it, even though that now sounds to me like a hopeless negation of what life offers – a sin in itself – and so I found myself leaving the world that I had known since childhood but never feeling I could belong completely to any other that wasn't shaped by some evident moral code. And the moral code wasn't about sin and punishment but rather something as vague as trying to do the right thing and not shutting yourself down to spiritual possibilities, wherever and however they could be found. But whichever way I try to explain it, it felt as if I lived then in my own self-created limbo, unable to connect to my own happiness because I didn't fully know in which world it might be grasped or how I might journey there.

So although it feels embarrassing to reveal, and possibly even difficult to believe, I went to Saigon and left it in the same virginal state. All around me were some of the most beautiful women I had ever seen, whether they wore the traditional ao dais or skimpy Westernised clothes. There were, too, the wealthy women with recently Westernised eyes that you saw window-shopping in the expensive Eden Arcade who exuded a superiority to all those around them and who wouldn't deign to glance sideways at such as me. But you couldn't be an American in Saigon for very long before someone came on to you willing to trade themselves for as many dollars as they might get. And of course there were times when I was tempted, times when I came close, but always I wanted something more than I knew I would get and I was frightened to do what I thought was a bad thing both for me and for them. If someone had offered me love, I would have grasped it with both hands, but what

I couldn't do was disfigure that desire for what ultimately was an economic exchange. And I hated what I saw so often in that city – pretty, petite women hanging on the arms of much older, pot-bellied American contractors with coarse hands and mouths; young women with smack-deadened eyes needing you only for a fix; girls hustling with the learned and obscene language of the street. As much as physically I wanted the experience, there was always something even stronger holding me back.

As for Corley, although we never spoke about it, I think he wasn't much more experienced than I was. He had a girlfriend back home called Sylvia, carried a picture of her in his wallet and corresponded on a continual basis. The young woman in the photo was blonde and pretty and he seemed smitten with her and intended asking her to marry him as soon as he had finished his tour. So together, at least, we never did anything about women, didn't even talk much about them but simply looked as we sat in downtown cafés or round the pool at Le Cercle Sportif. Sometimes when he saw someone he considered particularly stunning he'd blow a quiet stream of air that momentarily rose then dropped his fringe or let his fingers tap against the side of his glass. And that was it as far as I ever saw. What he thought about my lack of engagement I don't know. I guess now, like Meaulnes, I was looking for the woman I had fallen in love with, the only difference being that I hadn't actually met her and yet I was able to conjure constantly what such a meeting would be like and how my life would be, continually playing out romantic scenarios in my head. And nothing in the bars or street corners of Saigon promised anything that would replicate that creation of my imagination.

Once, poolside, Corley talked about writing – it amused me to hear him refer to himself as a writer on the basis of his stuttering attempts to produce a novel.

'I've been thinking about Hemingway,' he told me, 'and Steinbeck. Do you know what the difference is between them and us?' And when I took too long to ponder his pretty ludicrous question he replied, 'The biggest and most important difference, Michael, is that they wrote their books out of experience. Know what I mean? Both of them lived lives – did you ever read the number of jobs Steinbeck had? Ranch hand, carpenter, newspaperman – I can't remember them all – roving across America, and Hemingway's the same. So when they came to write they had so much stuff to draw on.'

He paused to try and find some decent music on the radio he had brought with him but eventually had to concede defeat. I took the opportunity to poke him a little.

'But, Corley, a novel is a work of the imagination. You don't need to have done things to have an imagination.'

He mussed the front of his hair as if I had hurt his brain and then, pulling his legs up towards himself, told me, 'Yes, but the imagination has to have something to turn to. You need water in the well – something to draw on. I think that's my problem. I've got nothing to draw on.'

'But we're here in a war in a foreign country, in the happening of history,' I told him. 'That must count for water in the well.'

'It should do but I don't think my war counts for very much. Or yours, for that matter. We're just shuffling paper, making up poor stories for someone else to tell.'

'So you'd rather have been hunkered up in some foxhole in the Central Highlands fighting off Charlie?'

'No, of course not, but if I had been, at least I'd know what it's like to be fully alive in the moment because I guess that's what it must feel like when faced with the reality of death. Sometimes, Michael, I think I'm just sleepwalking through my life and I know I'm never going to write my novel until I'm able to wake up.'

Then he fell silent for a while, as if exhausted by his self-dramatising efforts, and we went back to shyly studying the young women who paraded poolside.

I spent time with Corley because there wasn't anyone else, but I don't think we would have been particularly close friends in any other context. I liked him well enough, and he never did me any harm, but there was something unsatisfactory in him that occasionally irritated me. He came from a comfortable background – his father dealt in art in New York and his mother ran some kind of acting school. And whether it was because of that safety net, that silver spoon, there was a listlessness, a vagueness of purpose about him sometimes that got under my skin. My parents hadn't been able to give me much more than a faith I no longer wanted, so I'd worked hard at college, avoided all distractions, taken casual employment in a downtown store where I sold gardening equipment to help pay my way. And if I liked to think that I had the virtue of steadiness, even though I understand now that it often became a form of passivity where I allowed my life just to happen rather than trying to shape it, then it seemed to me that Corley drifted on the wind like a seed head, fastening on whatever idea or course of action that momentarily offered him a place to settle. But when these thoughts prevailed I felt, too, a sense of guilt because I knew that without him I would have been solitary, without the benefit of a guide however faulty and incomplete the map he possessed.

I saw that people occasionally found us amusing when we were out and about, so there were moments when it felt like we were the two uncool kids in class, against whom the others were able to assert their superiority. And even though we secretly thought that we were above it, at times I wanted him to speak in a less affected way in front of others, not be so keen to let himself be carried on a wave of enthusiasm, not be so quick to offer assertive judgements on whatever was under discussion. And once I betrayed him. It was at some event in the Embassy grounds, the type of event to which neither of us normally ever got invited, held to mark an occasion I can't remember, and Corley found himself holding forth to a group of women and I watched as he got pumped up on his own sense of insight into how the war should be brought to an end. He'd had a few drinks and was growing too loud.

'Is he a friend of yours?' a plain-clothes security guy asked.

'No, not really,' I answered.

'Because if he is, you need to tell him to tone it down.'

'It's the drink talking.'

'Then he needs to stop drinking. There's a time and place, and on the Ambassador's lawn is not the place to spill your guts. What's his name?'

'I think it's Corley Rodgers.'

'Corley fucking Rodgers. I should have known.'

Then he left me and I watched as he walked to where Corley was in full flow, regaling his audience with stories of supposedly ludicrous ineptitude associated with his job, saw him politely but firmly tap Corley on the shoulder and then lead him away, having first removed the wine glass from his hand. Soon afterwards I made my own retreat, a disloyal defector in my imagination, or one of those ghost soldiers who never fully existed.

When I was presented with an unscheduled opportunity for home leave, I turned it down. However, after hostilities resumed in open fury, and the Peace Accords seemed nothing more than just another worthless piece of paper, the atmosphere in Saigon edged with something darker than I had previously known and the volume of work entering our offices increased on a daily basis. We took more precautions about our personal security and soon loudspeakers in Lam Son Square were playing martial music. And then one Monday morning, just after I arrived for work, Greenberg summoned me to his office.

'I've had a phone call,' he said, standing in front of his plants with a small watering can in his hands. 'You're wanted in the Embassy. Report there to an agent called Donovan.' As I turned to go, he added in almost a fatherly way, 'Be careful, Michael.'

I paused for further elucidation, but none was forthcoming and he returned to the nurture of his orchids. The immediacy of the order spurred me to take a taxi, a beat-up blue and yellow Renault whose driver attempted a half-hearted extortion on the fare but capitulated at my first protest. Apart from that time with Corley, I had only been in the Embassy for one social function shortly after my arrival, and believed that having done their bit they had removed my name from the list of those meriting further hospitality.

It was obvious from the number of Marines on duty and the extra defences that security had been beefed up and it took me a while to reach the upper floors of the building where the CIA were based. I was increasingly nervous, wondering if I had screwed something up or whether my services were to be dispatched elsewhere. For a few seconds as I sat in a waiting area I even considered the possibility that one of my parents had died and I had been summoned to officially receive the news. I sat for about twenty minutes, and every single person who passed me, male or female, inspected me, registering a face that wasn't familiar. No one deigned to speak, and the chorus of clicking typewriters and people hurrying in the corridor holding sheaves of paper or cups of coffee gave it the impression of some corporate headquarters rather than the heart of covert operations. I realised later that Donovan was one of those who had passed me several times, but he hadn't introduced himself, and it was only when he called me by name that I understood he was the person I was to meet with.

Much of what I came to know about Ignatius Donovan accrued incrementally over the months that were to come, so on this first meeting I knew nothing about him except what I saw standing in front of me and what he bothered to reveal. Of average height but broad in the shoulders and probably aged in his mid to late thirties, he looked like a man who could push open a shut door and the expression on his face created the impression that he was permanently willing to do so, and in fact would have preferred that means of gaining entry as opposed to merely turning the handle. He had a sandy-haired crew cut and, despite the paleness of the rest of his skin, was red-faced, splenetic as if he'd stood too long looking up at the sun. He had a habit, too, of sniffing and on that first encounter and in the absence of a handshake it felt as if he was evaluating me by scent.

'Michael Miller?' he asked and, when I nodded, requested my ID.

He inspected it longer than seemed necessary, even looking at me in a way that suggested he was verifying the photograph in case I was an impostor; then, without introducing himself, turned on his heels and silently beckoned me to follow him. Along the corridor he stopped to glance into various offices, but clearly none of them offered what he was looking for and, turning to me, he said, 'We'll take a stroll, Mr Miller, shoot the breeze as we walk.'

He subsequently told me none of this but in the months to come I learned that he was a senior CIA analyst, Boston Irish, third-generation police who wanted to expand on his traditional family pathway and who had graduated with some distinction from the Foreign Service to his present post. He assumed I too was an Irish Catholic and looked at me in seeming disbelief when later in conversation it came out that I was a Presbyterian and my family's origins were from the north of Ireland rather than the south. I remember the moment clearly because for a second I thought he was going to throw me over and as he sniffed a couple of times it was if the smell of betrayal was in his nostrils. I almost apologised but instead made a joke about our ancestors both fleeing the Penal Laws. He didn't laugh or even smile and for a couple of days it felt as if he was reassessing me, weighing up whether his unexpected discovery made any difference to things.

But on that morning we walked and eventually ended up in an almost empty café where we took a table in a shaded corner.

'So you must have worn a good shine on the seat of your pants by now,' he said in between sipping his coffee and still inspecting me in an undisguised way that was unsettling and left me nervously thinking of an appropriate answer. When I said nothing in reply, he paused a little before saying, 'You're going to be working for me, helping where and how you're needed, and whatever that is doesn't get shared with anyone else. You understand?'

'Yes … ' and not knowing what to call him I added the word 'sir'. Then, as he silently evaluated that response, I asked, 'What about Mr Greenberg?'

'Greenberg's a daisy, the prom queen of the desk jockeys. He doesn't count for shit so don't you give him a second thought. You think that when Charlie starts flooding down Highway One Greenberg'll be the man to stand in his way?'

'No.'

'Damn right he won't, and when the shit hits the fan, and believe me it's going to hit it pretty soon, you won't see the likes of Nathaniel Greenberg for considerable dust. So the Service, your country, needs whatever skills you claim to have and needs you to stand up straight. Straight and true. You understand?'

I said I did without having any grasp of what I was needed for, and too intimidated to ask openly, and for a moment wondered if he had got me confused with someone else and hadn't realised by aptitude and nature I was nothing more than a desk jock. But the best I could venture was, 'I work a desk, basically. Sometimes a bit of translation.'

'I know what you do. You're not getting parachuted into Hanoi – I just need your services from time to time and a little back-watching, a little bag-carrying. That's all. When

I need you, you'll hear from me, and in the meantime don't discuss this conversation with anyone. And when Greenberg asks you, just tell him that you're needed to offer some unspecific additional support. Got it?'

'Yes, sir.'

'You're not on parade, Mikey. If you have to call me anything, you can address me as Mr Donovan. Most people call me Iggy but you're not most people yet. Hopefully you will be once I see you shape up.'

He paid our bill and I had a brief glimpse of a photograph in his wallet – a dark-haired woman with her arms round two small children. When we emerged from the shadows of the café into the light of the morning I blinked and raised my hand to shade my eyes, so for a second it must have looked like I was saluting him. Then, without any elaborate farewell, he was gone and I was left to make my journey back to my desk and when, as he had predicted, Greenberg gently enquired about the meeting, I responded in the way I had been instructed. I could see that this response wasn't very satisfactory to him but he didn't probe any further and instead turned on his heels with the air of a man who had been snubbed, leaving me to ponder what 'back-watching' would entail. Nor did I have any glimmer of awareness about the role that Donovan would subsequently come to play in my life. Perhaps if I had, things might have followed a different course.

That same night I received my second summons. This time it was from Madame Binh, who intercepted my arrival back at the apartment block with a wordless gesture to follow her through her open door. The first thing I registered was the smell of incense that lent everywhere a sickly scent. The room we stood in was furnished with mostly heavily lacquered pieces and the couch was covered with a kind of thick cellophane as if it was being kept good. An ornately carved screen with white cranes flying across it designated the separation of living space and kitchen. Still without speaking, she offered me a glass of a clear liquid she had already poured and, when I hesitated, said, 'Yes, yes,' and set me an example by draining her own.

'Snake wine very good for you,' she told me after I had emptied my glass and too late for me to wonder if it was such a good idea. 'Good for all things inside. Good for manhood.'

I began to think how best to take my leave without giving too much offence, but she was already pointing me to a small card table which had two chairs and I don't remember whether it was a relief or a new worry when she announced she was going to tell my fortune.

'I do it for all Americans who come here. There is no charge,' she said, and after she'd gestured me to sit, we looked at each other across the table. This was the closest I had ever been to her and I realised that she could have been sixty or eighty. Whichever, the age of her face was optimistically offset by a splash of rouge in the hollows of her cheek and her incredibly long nails were painted the brightest red. She wore a black, possibly silk trouser suit and her silver sandals revealed toenails of the same intense colour. Over her shoulder I saw another table that was decorated like a shrine, with some black and white silver-framed photographs, lit incense sticks, blossoms of jasmine in a glass bowl and a small golden Buddha.

I had to tell her my name, the day, month and year of my birth, and as she mulled over their significance I half-hoped that Corley would appear in the doorway and tell me that we needed to be somewhere, but all that broke the silence was the chirp of a yellow bird in a cage that stood near the window. When my birth details failed to elicit the necessary results, she began to study my face intensely and once stretched her hand across the table to test the outline of my chin. For a second I wondered if she might inspect my teeth but her hand dropped away and reached for a little canister containing thin bamboo sticks with writing on them. I had to shake them like dice but clumsily spilled nearly all and, getting a scolding, had to repeat it until one landed on the table. Lifting it, she deciphered my fortune from its hieroglyphics.

'You will enjoy long life,' she said. 'Good long life and good fortune.'

'That's very good,' I said, wondering if this was the sum total of my reading and thinking it might permit my departure.

'But you will never go home,' Madame Binh continued. 'Always your heart stays here. And you must beware deep water. Beware deep water and those who want to take your wealth when you least expect it. And your children will be girls only.'

Then she brought her hands together and bowed her head, and replicating the gesture I thanked her and, with the scent of incense still clinging to me, took my leave. It was the only time I have ever had my fortune told, and as predictions go it seemed pretty innocuous, so the only thing that stayed with me was not the idea of thieves in the night but never going home. But if I was to enjoy long life it meant I wasn't going home in a flag-draped box and I thought, despite my natural scepticism, that was something to hold on to, except when I later told Corley about having my fortune read he was able to predict that, like him and everyone else in the block, our future involved both never going home and long life.

Shortly after this encounter I did my first job for Donovan. He picked me up close to the end of the working day in a Ford Pinto and we drove to a restaurant called La Porte Bleue that was on the waterfront and which sat in a row dominated by closed-down clubs given sexy names and lurid drawings to attract GIs, uninviting bars and other small restaurants claiming to sell food from various parts of the world. As he drove I looked at the river that was a disappointing colour of days-old coffee, and the shadowy craft that plied its length had little elegance but seemed mostly to consist of hulking rust buckets, or smoking barges loaded with what seemed like cargoes of piled pottery. The river's dark skin was patched with eddies and in time I would come to know that it only assumed a mystery when glazed by the city's lights. Donovan didn't say much and when I tried small talk to avoid the embarrassment of silence he made little response.

La Porte Bleue didn't have a blue door and, apart from the few tables outside that hosted some card-playing smokers, didn't conform much to any of the impressions I held of a Parisian café. There was a faded mural along one wall with what might have been the artist's imagined vision of a lavender-drenched landscape but was more Italian than French in feel. The tables had blue chequered cloths and stubs of candles in ceramic bowls. Inside there were about a dozen customers, including two Americans with two Vietnamese women. Donovan exchanged a handshake with someone I assumed was the owner and introduced me to him as 'Mikey Boy'. I followed him through the restaurant and into a back room that looked as if it was reserved for special functions or private parties. There was a door at the end that opened into a darkened corridor and which might have led into living quarters. When Donovan sat at a table I took a seat also but he pointed me to the adjoining table, saying, 'Need a little space, don't want to crowd anyone.' A woman entered with two bottles of beer on a tray and Donovan stood to greet her politely, then as an afterthought introduced me. She was probably in her mid-forties, with her hair pinned up and held in place with what looked like a silver clasp and elegantly dressed in a cream-coloured ao dai. Her name was Quyen and she bowed her head to me in greeting and smiled, then she was gone.

'She owns the place with Vien. It's passed down through the family since the French. A good spot to eat,' Donovan said, taking his first sip of beer.

But we hadn't come to eat and a few minutes later a Vietnamese man entered and sat at the same table as Donovan, then proceeded to stare at me until he was told not to worry, that I was an assistant.

'Get our friend a beer,' Donovan told me and I went back out into the restaurant where Quyen served me from the bar. The two Americans were having their photographs taken by Vien, their heavy, gold-braceleted arms resting like yokes across the shoulders of their companions. I saw Quyen looking at them as she poured the beer, but her face revealed nothing of her thoughts and when she smiled for me it was tired and never reached her eyes. When I returned to the back room Donovan was in some kind of bargain-making with the man.

'Yes, whole family out. Sure, no problem on that but not yet. I need more, I need you here for more, just for a little while longer. There'll be visas for every last one. No problem. You understand?'

The man nodded unenthusiastically and placed both hands palm downwards on the table in a gesture that seemed to say he had no more cards to play.

'Mikey, take notes,' Donovan said, and when I told him I didn't have a notebook he looked at me with scorn then took a small black book and pen out of his jacket pocket and threw them to me. For the next thirty minutes I recorded information about military build-ups in specific locations, the supposed morale and intentions of particular ARVN generals and the infiltration into Saigon of Vietcong cadres and agents. But towards the end of the interview Donovan pressed his source on information being relayed to someone called Bloomfield and it was in those moments that he became most animated, often dissatisfied by the given responses and shaking his head in disbelief. Then, as the interview wound to an end, he resumed his former ebullient manner and, with a final slap on the back, sent his informant into the night, his ears ringing with more promises of future benevolence.

'The skill, Mikey, now is deciding which parts were bullshit and which worth pinning your name to,' he said as he took the notebook from me and perused its contents.

'Who's Bloomfield?' I asked.

'One slippery son of a bitch, that's who he is.'

There was no further elaboration and, when Vien appeared in the doorway and asked if we wanted to eat, Donovan declined. But just before we were about to leave, a young woman I assumed was the owners' daughter emerged from the private quarters and Donovan greeted her with the same politeness he had reserved for her mother. She was called Tuyen and she had inherited her mother's looks and then some.

At this point in a Saigon story I fall hopelessly in love, willing to throw over everything if it brings me her hand. That's not in fact my story, although perhaps in another telling it could well have been, and on that first meeting I did nothing but try not to look longer than was polite. She had a self-contained sense of detachment about her that both attracted and discouraged. You knew she wasn't ever going to appear on the arm of some contractor, whatever the size of his wallet. And as we walked back through the restaurant I heard Donovan say, 'Put your eyeballs back in, Mikey. You'd be pitching far out of your league.'

In the car he told me that the family had worked for the French, that Quyen herself was mixed race and Tuyen had been educated in a French school in Saigon. Then, after a silence settled and we were approaching my apartment block, for some reason – perhaps in an attempt to assert a sense of my independent thought – I asked him again who Bloomfield was and, with wordless exasperation, he stopped the car and parked up alongside a tattoo parlour, and all these years later I may have misremembered the permutations he sought to educate me in.

'Bloomfield is an intelligence officer for DAO, although I hesitate to use his name in the same sentence as intelligence. Works out of Tan Son Nhut,' he said, then paused as if uncertain whether to continue or not. 'OK, Mikey, as you're going to work for me, we'll get this straight. We are here, right? Washington is there, right?' I tried to preserve my dignity by not responding. 'What gets decided there largely gets decided on what they get told here. Bloomfield answers to Bill LeGro who answers to General Homer Smith who answers to Military Command. Military Command answers to Washington which occasionally has to answer to Congress. I, rather we, answer to Polgar, Section Chief, who, despite what anyone else says or thinks, answers to Langley. You understand? And then there's the Southern son of a bitch Ambassador Graham Martin. You've met him?' I shook my head. 'No, of course not, why would he want to meet cotton pickers like you or me? And I think he's one of you lot, a Baptist or something.'

When he didn't continue, but seemed to change his attention to the tattoo parlour, I asked, 'And who does the Ambassador answer to?'

'The Ambassador answers only to God, Mikey, and not even then when God doesn't tell him what he wants to hear. The Ambassador is the man who's going to get you killed because he doesn't want to be the man who lowers the flag. And he lost a son here, so it's personal. There's a saying – the sheep fear the wolves but it's the shepherd who kills them. And that's what we're talking about here. All of us killed by the shepherd.'

There was a moment of silence then he asked if I'd ever got a tattoo. When I told him I hadn't, he rolled up his sleeve and showed me a shamrock with the words 'Mum' and 'Dad' on either side of the stem. As his jacket opened I saw the butt of his holstered gun and knew enough to recognise it as a .38-calibre Smith & Wesson.

'Not very sophisticated, I know, but when you're young you sometimes make bad decisions. My old man went crazy, threatened to whip my sorry ass. He did that a lot until he knew he couldn't do it any more. And I'd done it to please him. That's what got me.'

He fell silent for a second, as if scrutinising some past memory, then rolled his sleeve back down.

'Your old man must be proud of you, Mikey. Ivy League boy. No bad habits.'

'He found other things to be disappointed in. Fathers always do, I guess.'

'Ain't that the truth. Ain't that the truth. When we watched the moon landings, my old man sat with a can of beer in his hand in his undershirt, just like he did every night he came off duty, and you know what he said?'

I shook my head.

'"Hell of a long way to go to know what loneliness feels like." Can you believe that, Mikey? "Hell of a long way to go to know what loneliness feels like." That's exactly what he said.'

Then we sat in silence for a few seconds more as we contemplated the meaning of his father's words, until he broke the spell by slapping the steering wheel with the palm of his hand. Before I got out of the car he handed me a document he wanted translated from French and asked me, 'Has Madame Binh told your fortune yet?' As he put the engine in gear he started to laugh and his final words were, 'She got mine all wrong.' Then he was gone, the car's lights fading rapidly into the dusk.

Within a relatively short time I began to understand that Donovan's war was in some part a deeply personal one and he waged it mostly against George Bloomfield, who I had never met but came to feel as if I had. And when Donovan spoke of him he invariably did so in pyrotechnic language that involved such assertions as he was going to light a fire under that son of a bitch's ass, tie a firecracker to his tail or smoke him out once and for all. Why he hated Bloomfield so intensely was never revealed to me, but from different sources I heard a range of suggestions, everything from Donovan holding the other responsible for the betrayal and subsequent death of one of his most valued agents, to a protracted and bitter dispute over a woman. There was even talk of a fist fight in the bar of the Caravelle Hotel. But whatever the reason behind their enmity, it conspired to dominate much of his thinking and I came to believe that Donovan's most pressing motivations were to put one over his nemesis and to ensure that his analyses were the primary influences on Polgar's and the station's current thinking.

Despite Donovan warning me that Tuyen was off limits, opportunities arose for me to at least get to know her a little better. One Sunday afternoon when I was playing tennis with Corley at Le Cercle Sportif, a complex that was to eventually assume the august title of the Ho Chi Minh City Labour Culture Palace, Tuyen appeared with a female friend – it transpired later that Donovan had secured their entry. And I know that with all the cinematic cultural reimagining of the war, the smell of napalm in the morning and full metal jackets et cetera, the idea of Sunday-afternoon tennis probably seems bizarre, but this was a part of my experience because I had arrived initially in that period when both sides were pretending peace was what they desired rather than victory. I had missed much of the worst attrition and would be gone soon after the storm finally broke.

When I saw Tuyen and her companion in immaculate whites, I was embarrassed by our makeshift tennis gear but she seemed friendly and, as she was playing on the court beside ours, there were lots of times when mishit shots ended on the wrong court. I probably hit more wayward shots than normal because I was distracted by her presence, and my constant glances revealed that she was a good player, deceptively languid in her movements but able to serve with precision and pace, able to both drive and slice the ball elegantly on her backhand. After a while, when our change of ends coincided, she asked me if we wanted to play doubles and at first I thought she meant she and her partner would play against us but she gestured with her racquet that she would play with me. So we paired off, introductions were made, and while I knew Corley was impressed by my knowing her I was conscious that, if anything, he looked even scruffier than me in his canvas baseball shoes and cut-off denim shorts.

But we all played with a display of commitment, even managed a few sustained rallies, and raising my own game, I suppose in a desire to impress, I eventually secured our win with a neat volley at the net. Afterwards we had drinks on the terrace and I was able to shut Corley out by chatting to Tuyen in French, but not before I heard him tell her companion that he was a writer. And, despite everything, Corley possessed a boyish charm that could be attractive when he wasn't agonising about Sylvia or some other aspect of his life, so my conversation with Tuyen took place to the accompaniment of frequent laughter from Tuyen's friend.

She asked me about my job and I told her as much and as little as was permissible while probably ensuring that the air of secrecy with which I described it gave it a romantic edge and inflated its significance without ever telling outright lies. I also exaggerated my relationship

49

with Donovan but when I made a couple of mild jokes at his expense she didn't laugh and instead gave me one of her fleeting smiles that, as always, left me uncertain as to what she was thinking. She wanted to become a teacher, she said, perhaps travel abroad, and she asked me if I'd ever been to Paris. It was pretty impossible, even without the benefit of imagination, to suggest I was some kind of well-travelled cosmopolitan rather than a small-town prairie boy, and more than once I remembered Donovan's assertion that I was pitching out of my league. But even as we sat together I didn't consider that I was actually pitching because, despite the pleasure I found in her company, at constantly looking at her but trying not to stare, I never really rated myself highly enough to think my prospects amounted to very much. Despite our intellectual pretensions, Corley and I were water-carriers, camp followers of Uncle Sam, so face to face with her beauty and what I thought of as her sophistication, even in the way she lit and held her cigarette, I felt only the weight of my unworldly inadequacy.

There was one more game of tennis on a Sunday afternoon, followed again by drinks, but little accrued from these encounters other than some unspoken and unshared wishful thinking on my part and boyish fantasies that always took place in Paris. And I never really knew who she was, and even though she must have been about the same age as me there always seemed an important part of her that was private, a part that I never got to see and which she never chose to reveal. In a way that suited me because I was able to construct her in the image that best matched my ideal.

There was only one time when I caught a brief glimpse of another, more vulnerable and perhaps more real person rather than that ideal. I had been to La Porte Bleue with Donovan for a meeting with someone he hoped would be useful. If anything he was more tetchy than usual, his irritation with me undisguised, as if I was guilty of some failure even though I had no idea what it was I was supposed to have done, but then I saw that he was on edge with everyone who came near him. He was also drinking more than usual and with a frequency that spoke of a darkening mood. Once when he had finished a beer he rattled the bottle noisily on the table to summon service and when Tuyen brought him another he never looked at her or offered thanks. A few minutes later he told me to go and keep an eye on the car – there was obviously some part of his conversation he didn't want me to hear and when he spoke to me his tone was dismissive, edged with disdain. As if he was speaking to a minion. I could happily have told him to find someone else to mind his car, but I didn't, glad to be out of his presence. And that was something I already understood about Donovan – he had the power to make you feel negatively about yourself, about whatever he supposed your momentary inadequacy was, and it often smarted like a paper cut to your pride and the sense of your own dignity, even if you were eventually able to salve the cut and restore your self-respect. Turn the feelings into a renewed resentment towards him.

I stood just outside the entrance and it was a few seconds before I saw Tuyen huddled in a closed doorway nearby. The smoke from her cigarette lifted itself lazily into the night. Out on the river small boats made mysterious journeys, with solitary yellow lights warning other craft of their presence. A group of men sitting on packing cases and in white shirts were playing a dice game under the spreading branches of a tree. From time to time their voices rose in cheers or what sounded like curses. When I approached her I saw that she was crying and I didn't know whether to speak to her or respect her privacy, but she offered me a cigarette and, even though I must have been one of the very few who had come through adolescence without ever smoking, I accepted. Accepted, then made a fool of myself by spluttering and almost choking, but at least it served momentarily to distract from whatever it was Tuyen was upset about, because she smiled at my discomfort. When I recovered some composure I asked her if she was OK and in reply she simply nodded. I was about to leave her and return to my car-watching duty when she flicked her cigarette into the shadows and told me I was very kind. I knew she meant kind in comparison to Donovan, who I guessed was the cause of her discomfort. But I never really believed that I would ever be the bestower of anything other than minor kindness or the recipient of more than casual conversation.

There were other distractions, with moments of unexpected brightness, even when things started to darken in Saigon. I had already been invited to a Tet celebration at Danh's family home, a riotous occasion that contrasted with my own family's austere Thanksgivings, and a short while later I received an embossed invitation to his wedding. It took place in a side chapel of the Notre-Dame Cathedral – it was the first time I had ever been in any place of worship other than the one in which I had grown up and it was a strange experience sitting under that vaulted ceiling and absorbing so much that was different to all I had been accustomed to. And despite the warmth of the occasion, the unfamiliar and, to my eyes at least, gaudy iconography made me uneasy. I know the importance of religious iconography in the sustenance of faith and by the end of this story would come to understand it in a better way, even though my Presbyterian upbringing has done its best to ingrain a reverence for the plain, the unadorned. But I've been in enough yellow taxis where drivers of many different faiths hang their religious talismans from rear-view mirrors, or decorate the dashboard, to know there's a very thin line between faith and superstition. In more recent times the cathedral would provide its own 'miracle' when worshippers claimed to have seen the statue of the Virgin Mary shed a tear, causing thousands of believers to flock to the site, ardent to see the weeping mother of Christ. But the closest they probably came to a tear was through buying one of its postcard images hot off the presses.

I felt a stranger inside Notre-Dame but also that it represented the painted backdrop to Donovan's world and so was part too of the glaring disconnection between what was supposedly believed and what was done, and how the orbits of these two separate worlds never seemed destined to touch. But all such metaphysical speculation faded quickly because after the Catholic ceremony there was another, more traditional one, followed by a banquet at a restaurant where I lost count of the courses and where everyone seemed to have access to a natural joy that made me feel both at ease and conscious that it felt so strange. The happiness of the newly-wed couple permeated the room and I hung back from them as if unwilling to come too close to what I wanted for myself in case, like some mirage, it vanished at the very moment it appeared most real.

Afterwards I walked home alone through the dusk and, as the wedding's vicarious happiness faded, felt an almost unbearable weight of loneliness. I passed bars where bored hookers hustled mechanically in doorways lit up by interior light so that they were momentarily transfigured, and wondered if it would take it away. Part of me wanted to believe it possible, and once I hesitated, paused for a second before moving on with the girls' taunts following me, including one that offered to introduce me to her 'very nice brother'. But to do the deed with one of the bar girls I knew I would have had to hate her and I knew it wasn't hatred I wanted to give or receive.

Saigon at night was communal in a way I had never known, with groups of people eating outside or gathered round improvised tables and the streets still flowing with the incessant flux of life, so to be solitary felt exposed and even vulnerable both physically and emotionally. And yet I didn't want to return to my apartment where I knew there would be no easy respite and so on impulse I turned and headed in the direction of La Porte Bleue, striding out with a purpose I didn't feel or understand. I passed ragged ribbons of huckster shops, some with glass cases on tables and their owners sprawled on bamboo furniture behind them; street cafés under striped awnings and above them shadowy people moving on balconies hung with washing; and narrow side streets where the evening heat smouldered undeterred and long rows of parked motorbikes and scooters lazed silently under trees. As I walked along the river the city lights sheened away some of its ugliness and momentarily allowed the possibility of mystery despite the shanty dwellings that laced the bank. But I walked too quickly to linger and, when I strode through the various huddled groups of families eating their evening meals or playing card games, they looked up at me with startled faces. Perhaps just for a second my white face resembled that of a ghost, leaving even the children too confused to follow with outstretched hands. Only a barking dog managed to muster a brief response.

The closer I got to my destination, the more uncertain I was as to my purpose, and when the restaurant eventually came into view I paused for the first time. At that distance the framed yellow square of light betrayed little of what passed inside, while the cigarette ends of those sitting outside hovered languidly in the dusk like fireflies. I was about to go closer when a car pulled up – a Ford Pinto – and Tuyen got out, briefly bowing her head to speak to the driver before she disappeared into the restaurant and the car moved off. There was a tug at my elbow. A young girl about seven or eight years of age was holding her hand out. I remembered the photograph in Donovan's wallet. The girl tugged my sleeve again and I stuck a dollar in her hand and turned the way I had come, trying to be uncertain of the significance of what I'd seen.

I found Corley sitting on the entrance's front steps in shorts and listening to Harry Chapin on his transistor radio, one hand flicking at insects, the other trying to angle the aerial to catch the best reception.

'How was the wedding?' he asked.

'Good,' I said, 'but thought it would never end. They really go all out. It'll be your turn next.'

But Corley seemed more subdued than usual and when he didn't reply I sat down on the steps beside him.

'She's not sure about getting married – I've kind of vaguely floated the idea. Says she thinks it might be too soon. That she has a career and I need to be settled back home before we go ahead.'

'We'll all be going home pretty soon,' I told him.

'How can it be too soon when we've been going out together since high school?'

'She just needs you home. Everything will be fine.'

'Absence is supposed to make the heart grow fonder. Maybe I need to earn a medal or something, or take one for Uncle Sam. A flesh wound preferably.'

His joke seemed to lift his spirits a bit and as we sat listening to the radio he let himself slip into a Corley riff.

'So, Michael, fellow man of the world, you think I'm not about to get a Dear John letter?' And when I told him no, 'And you're sure that Sylvia isn't going to be swept off her feet by some Tom Buchanan she's working with, some geography-teaching Tom Buchanan wooing her with his globes, or a Charles Atlas gym instructor who thinks human achievement is how many dumb-bell lifts you can do.'

'That's not going to happen,' I told him as convincingly as I could and then thought of Tuyen getting out of Donovan's car and knew that, despite what I had said, there was nothing that was impossible. In an attempt to distract both of us from our darker thoughts, I asked, 'How's the novel going?'

'Not good.' There was a pause and I wasn't sure if he was going to elaborate or not but, as Harry Chapin's 'W.O.L.D.' turned into the Steve Miller Band and 'The Joker', he continued, 'I think it's my day job. Before, I wrote only good stories and now I have to write only bad ones about what happens when Charlie takes over your village town or city, and I don't know any more what's true and what's made up. Know what I mean?' I nodded even though I didn't. 'And then when I write the novel, I'm writing what isn't true because that's what fiction is, but at the same time it has to be true or it has no value. So different parts of my brain are doing different things and I don't know which one I'm supposed to be listening to.'

At this point most young men would probably have smoked some dope or gone downtown, got drunk and laid, but for different, and not always easily explained, reasons these options didn't seem open to us and so in their place we decided, when we could borrow a car, we'd travel out to the beach resort of Vung Tau and attempt our own boyish version of R&R, have a swim in the sea. It seemed important for us to get out of the city that, as rumour and fears tightened around it, had started to feel constrained, even claustrophobic at times, so there were moments when to my surprise I sensed a fleeting nostalgia for the world of the prairie. But before that excursion happened there was work to be done and in the following days I was inundated with a seemingly endless flow of documents that originated from various sources, including one inside the French Embassy itself which focused on clandestine French negotiations with the North Vietnamese. What their overall purpose was I couldn't say, other than perhaps a forlorn attempt to recover face and possibly restore some influence in the region as a whole. But it transpired Donovan had some ongoing interest in them and one day at the end of work he was waiting for me in his car a short distance along from the office building and there was nothing in the way of preamble.

'I need copies of the French documents – the ones coming in through the Embassy,' he said, sniffing a little and looking in the mirror then flattening the top of his crew cut with the palm of his hand.

'You'll need to ask Greenberg,' I said, happy to be unhelpful.

'I'm not asking Greenberg because if I do I won't get to see them. They're not coming through one of our channels and are destined for someone else's desk.'

'I can't show you anything without Greenberg's knowledge and permission. That's how it works. You must know that.'

'Listen, Mikey, the first time I met you I told you I needed you to stand up straight and true – you remember? Well this is one of those moments.'

But I gave him nothing back and he knew I wasn't persuaded so, turning full face to me, he said, 'I'm not asking you, Mikey, I'm telling you. It's an order.'

'Will you put it in writing?'

'No, I fucking won't put it in writing.' His face had flushed a darker shade of red. I imagined it closing in on Tuyen's face. 'Are you completely off your head? Have you forgotten who it is you're working for? Jeez, I'd like to spend five minutes with the asshole who thought you were up to this line of work.' He slapped the top of the steering wheel. 'Because, if you have forgotten, let me remind you it's not the fucking Boy Scouts. And this isn't summer camp.'

'How do I know it's a proper order and not just something you want to get one over on Bloomfield?'

'Bloomfield? What's Bloomfield got to do with it? This isn't about that patsy.'

'So what's it got to do with?'

He pushed himself back into the seat, making it squeak, and shook his head in exasperation then said, 'When I got landed with you, Mikey, I drew the short straw. You're sitting here safely pushing paper but, just in case you hadn't realised, there's a war out there and very soon it's going to be knocking on all our doors.' He momentarily ran out of steam and turned his head away to stare out his open window.

'Maybe you should stop treating me like an idiot,' I said, before I had time to consider whether it was wise or foolish.

There was only silence. I looked straight ahead and wondered what the consequences might be. A young woman in a conical hat approached Donovan's window, offering him a spray of flowers to buy. Suddenly he was screaming for me to get out, but before I could do that he had thrown his door open against the woman, knocking her backwards, and he was out of the car, the gun in his hand, and he was shouting at her to get down on the ground. For a second I thought he was going to shoot the now cowering woman, but instead he pushed his foot through the splayed bunch of flowers until satisfied there was nothing hiding there, then threw her some money and told me to get back in the car.

He started the engine without speaking.

'She works out of that kiosk,' I told him, pointing at it as we drove past.

He didn't reply but all his agitation flowed into his driving and his hand repeatedly hit the horn at all those who strayed into his path and were too slow in getting out of his way. For some reason he had driven us to Le Cercle Sportif and when he did speak the tenor of his voice had changed. Instead of that mocking humour he liked to employ, there was a quieter, more resigned tone and for the first time since we'd met he called me Michael.

'So, Michael, this is how it is. The war is lost – you don't need to have any doubts about that. And what remains now is for us, all of us, and that includes those Vietnamese who have done good work for us, to get out of here in one piece. And I don't know how long we've got but we have to be ready. You understand?'

I said I did and he nodded as if he was pleased.

'But we have a problem, and that problem is Martin and maybe even Polgar, and I'm talking to you man to man now – no bullshit. Martin still believes that a negotiated settlement is possible and part of Polgar wants to believe that too. They want to believe that, when everything out there says the very opposite and that Charlie's not going to stop until his flag's flowing over the presidential palace and his tanks are parked outside on the lawn. And the longer they go on believing that, the less time we have to get out of here with as many of our people as possible.'

'So how does this relate to the French documents you want?'

'I need everything I can find about the North's intentions. I just need any insight from as many credible sources as I can get my hands on that Charlie's not going to accept anything less than a military victory. Now I didn't need to tell you any of this but I have. So respect that.'

He asked me again if I understood and perhaps it was my concerns for the people who worked with me that made me tell him I'd get him what he wanted.

'So tomorrow mid-afternoon Greenberg will get a call that'll tell him he's needed to attend a meeting in the Embassy. That's when you'll do it.'

'He'll lock his office.'

'Yes he will and that's why I'm giving you this key,' he said as he handed it to me. 'These are the code numbers you're looking for. Make the copies in the room, take nothing original out. So you think you're ready to step off your desk and into the field? That's good, Mikey, and no need to thank me for saving your life.'

'Saving my life?'

'From the exploding flowers,' he said and then he laughed. 'Now I'm going for a swim. You can join me or have a drink and wait.'

Before he went to get out of the car I touched him lightly on his arm and, suddenly and uncharacteristically emboldened, said, 'It'll cost you.'

'Cost me?'

'Your car when I ask. We're going to Vung Tau. Swim in the sea.'

'I like it, Mikey. Always good to negotiate from a position of strength. And you got a hot date lined up, I assume.'

'I'm going with Corley Rodgers.'

'Roy Rodgers? Corley, Corley, Tell a Story Rodgers?'

He blew a loud stream of breath dismissively and stared at me, but I simply shrugged before telling him I'd look after the car. And a short time later I was sitting poolside with a cold drink watching him do lengths, his hair a splash of flame extinguishing itself each time it went under the water, the tattoo green in the sunlight as his arms rose and fell with a steady fury. But as his broad shoulders broke the surface I thought again of his body overpowering that of

Tuyen's and something tightened and sickened inside me. And I was frightened, too, about what I had agreed to do for him — it was something that was foreign to me and completely out of sync with my instinctive deference to whatever rules authority sought to create.

The following afternoon seemed to drag endlessly as I waited for Greenberg's phone call, and I started to hope that there had been some change of plan and that my involvement was no longer necessary. But at three o'clock exactly I heard Greenberg's phone ring and it sounded shriller and more insistent than ever before. A few minutes later I heard him emerging from his office and through the open door I glimpsed him carrying a briefcase and putting on his sunglasses. There was the barely perceptible sound of his lisping breathing and light footsteps on the stairs and then the room was silent again except for the turn of the ceiling fans and the creak of someone's chair. To my disappointment, my hand touched the cold metal of the key in my pocket, because part of me hoped to find that its presence was a figment of the imagination and that the task imposed on me had been nothing more than a stressful dream.

I looked around at my colleagues engrossed in their endless work and desks littered with piled-up in trays, sagging bulky rows of dictionaries, cassette players and headphones, and I knew that what I had to do had to be done right away or my doubts would leave me unable to go through with it. Lifting a bunch of papers, I walked past their desks, even exchanging greetings with some as I went, making a comment about how busy they were or contributing to some long-running office joke. I gently pulled the door after me, not enough to completely close it but enough to hide my right turn to Greenberg's office, even though I guessed his departure probably hadn't registered with most of them. I forced my hand steady and turned the key as quietly as possible and then, with a heart that seemed to drum so loudly it must betray my presence, I was in.

This moment of my first official deception. My first step into the field. But it didn't feel exciting or even manly – if anything, in my memory it assumes a meanness, a contraction of some part of who I thought I was. A small boy stealing apples from a neighbour's orchard? Cheating in an examination? I'd never done either of those things so perhaps that renders the comparisons meaningless. But whatever it was, as I quickly located the required documents I tried to exonerate myself by invoking that age-old get-out clause – what I did was for the greater good. I know now of course that the greater good is the most nebulous and malleable of concepts, and one that often allows us to proceed in the face of more precise, if often unwelcome truths. But I made the required copies, alarmed at the noise it unavoidably produced, and got out of the office where even the white orchids seemed to smoulder with accusation, then locked the door behind me. But I had only taken a few steps when I realised that the papers I now held didn't include the random collection I had carried in, and I flustered momentarily with the key, my hands suddenly clumsy. And the few seconds that it took to retrieve the papers reverberated with anticipation of discovery. Then, as I locked the door again while wondering about security that could be breached with a single key, I heard movement behind me. When I turned, Corrine was standing there but, as I struggled to think of what to say that might explain what I was doing, she simply lowered her eyes and headed back along the corridor.

Afterwards, as I sat at my desk, I thought my guilt must have been written large on my face and I glanced at her repeatedly, but throughout the office work carried on as normally and so I tried to concentrate on the translation in front of me. I watched a green lizard scurry across the ceiling above a window and dislodge a little flake of paint that fell slowly to earth like a solitary snowflake. Then, inexplicably, I experienced a fleeting feeling of giddiness and imagined transforming the document's leaden, plodding contents into something more fantastical – the Vietcong riding down the highway on elephants, the jungle sprouting hydra-headed monsters with diamonds for eyes – and wondered if anyone would actually take any notice before, with all the other things I had written, it was shredded and burnt in the incinerators that sprouted on rooftops everywhere our flag flew.

Later that evening, when I handed the requested documents to Donovan, I was disappointed by his lack of enthusiasm. But what had I expected – some effusive display of gratitude or a fatherly pat on the back? When I looked at him as he scanned their pages, he seemed shorn of his normal self and in his quiet introspection I thought that for the first time I glimpsed someone who existed under the surface of his usual buoyancy. And I wondered if the tough little Irish persona he exuded was just another form of disguise, a subterfuge intended to confuse any close surveillance of his person. It took him a long time to speak and when he did it was to tell me that I had done well, but it was obvious that what I had given him hadn't offered him the content he was looking for. Despite his subdued mood and my earlier speculation about his tough image being a pretence, I thought again of him swimming and remembered how, even in a yielding, giving element such as water, he had fought it as if seeking to impose his will incessantly. I pondered whether that constant expenditure of energy had now rendered him weary or even uncertain about what the coming days might bring. He slouched in his seat and wiped his mouth with the back of his hand. There were beads of sweat on his forehead.

'Are you OK?' I asked.

'Sure, Mikey,' he said.

'They didn't contain what you were looking for? What you needed?'

'It all helps – I wasn't expecting gold dust.'

'You sure you're OK?'

'What is this – the third degree?'

'You don't look well. You don't look yourself.'

'So now you're a doctor,' he said. 'You've only just become a player, done a little chickenshit thing, and now you think you're a doctor as well.'

But his irritation subsided almost as quickly as it had arisen and I knew too that something had altered in our relationship. I would still play the role of subservient – and in outward and practical matters that was what I was, even though I couldn't help feeling an intellectual superiority to him – but neither of us could entirely believe the other was a complete fool. While he continued to spar with me and occasionally offer his exasperated scorn, I think in the coming weeks he understood I could stand up if that was what was needed. And my involvement was increasingly required as I reprised my visit to Greenberg's office, and on some of those incursions I suspected that the requested material was destined for DAO and in particular George Bloomfield. On occasions, as instructed, I slipped documents into the burn bag that was destined for the incinerator and once I inserted a document that Donovan had given me, and for all I know that he had written, into a particular file. It struck me then, as it continues to do, how much energy must have been dissipated in this fragmented world of conflicted interests and power struggles. We were engaged in the dying throes of a war that had cost so many lives and yet there was no unity of political or military purpose, and strong-willed individuals and centres of power were allowed to continue imposing readings of events depending on their particular point of view or their vested self-interest. And when this was compared to the relentless unity of purpose displayed by our enemy, our ultimate defeat can hardly come as a surprise. But it's not as simple as that because, if you were to ask me, I would probably once have said that the very thing I thought of as our weakness stood as our national strength. So perhaps it is the multiplicity of unfettered voices that best allows us to be who we are. However, time and events change things and now so many bitterly discordant voices begin to proliferate I'm no longer sure it's a belief I still harbour.

There were other nights when I went with Donovan to La Porte Bleue to meet various contacts, and sometimes after sending me out to the bar he'd talk at length to Vien and Quyen and I'd hear the clink of glasses and occasionally laughter. I would sit at the bar and hope that Tuyen would find time to pause from her waitressing to talk with me, and there were intervals when she did. She liked to speak in French, saying she was glad to get a chance to practise, and I'd try to be witty, give my conversation as good an accent as hers as we engaged in small talk. At other times she was mostly out of sight or too busy to linger long. Once, when she was waitressing and Donovan was in the back room, a dispute over a bill broke out and in the mirror behind the bar I watched as two Americans who were with their Vietnamese girlfriends started giving her loud abuse about being ripped off and charged for what they hadn't had. She stood calmly, speaking so quietly that I could hardly hear what she was saying even as around her the voices grew louder. In the mirror I saw hands waving and pointing and a glass went over and shattered on the floor. I knew I had to intervene, but while I hesitated Donovan came out of the back room, followed by Vien, and with one hand he gently eased Tuyen to the side of him then placed his other on the table in a way that looked as if he was merely steadying a rickety piece of furniture. I got off the bar stool and tried to give the impression I was ready to assist. There was an argumentative American voice and then Donovan leaned in close to him, almost whispering in his ear, and no one but the man he was talking to could have heard what was being said before money was thrown on the table and the Americans made a hurried exit, a chair knocked over as they went and their Vietnamese consorts tottering after them with high heels clicking on the tiled floor. Afterwards, when he was driving me back to my apartment, I asked him what he had said but he only laughed before saying, 'On a need-to-know basis only, Mikey.'

We did a detour for some reason that wasn't explained and when we were driving past Notre-Dame he asked me if I ever went to church.

'Weddings and funerals mostly,' I told him.

'So you're not a believer.'

'I'm a believer but just not in all the things I used to.'

'It's a cold religion, Protestantism, anyway. Can't even warm itself with a candle.'

'Why do you say it's cold?'

'You've got all that burden of sin to carry on your shoulders.'

'And Catholics don't?'

'We have a get-out-of-jail card that never expires. Our spiritual PX pass that allows you back in the store with money to spend,' he said as he nosed the car through a phalanx of motorbikes. And when he saw that I didn't understand, 'Sin, confession, penance, followed by new sin. The joyous circle of life.'

And then, as the traffic momentarily clogged preventing our progress, I wanted to ask him about Tuyen and what penance could be done for what to me seemed like a very real sin, but I wasn't brave enough.

'Have you even experienced what's on offer in Saigon?' he suddenly asked, glancing at me. 'Maybe that's a sin would be good for you. We could go to the Miramar or even Mimi's, get you fixed up for the night. An old hand or an innocent fresh up from the country – your choice. What do you say? Get some of that starch out of your shirt. Help you lighten up, give you a clear head for what's about to come.'

I declined, frightened of what penance I would have to pay permanently, and he simply shrugged, making no further effort to persuade me. Outside my apartment block he stopped without turning off the engine and as I was getting out he said, 'Change your mind and I'll take care of things for you. Discretion part of the service.' Then he was gone, and for a few seconds I stood watching as black pulses of bats swooped into the emptiness of his wake.

I didn't get to leave Saigon without meeting my designated enemy face to face and in ways I had never anticipated. The first time was when I was summoned via Greenberg to meet Donovan close to our office.

'So he's found work for you,' Greenberg said as he told me about Donovan's phone call.

'Mostly just bag-holding,' I said, trying to look nonchalant. 'Nothing very spectacular.'

'And nothing dangerous, I hope,' he said, the final word a susurration that was almost part of his breathing.

'No, nothing dangerous,' I told him, anxious to be gone and increasingly conscious of my previous intrusions into the space we now shared.

'Danger follows men like Donovan. They attract it,' Greenberg said, looking intently at me. 'Sometimes I think they enjoy it because it allows them to be who they are. They need wars to thrive – it's their perfect environment. Don't you think?'

I didn't know what to say so gave a non-committal nod and when he said nothing more I turned to go.

'Michael, I told you once to be careful and I'm telling you again. I can't claim to know you well but I know enough to see that, like me, you're in the wrong place. And I don't know where your right place is, or whether like Meaulnes you'll struggle to find it, but it isn't here or with people like Donovan.'

'I know that,' I said and I thanked him, conscious even as I did of my betrayal.

Yet, as I walked out of the building that morning, I wondered if we were both wrong and whatever it was that existed in people like Donovan was a necessary force and its absence in us was the deficiency that would prevent us inheriting the earth, imposing on it any of the things we clung to and told ourselves were right. And as I headed to the corner where he stood smoking a cigarette, with his back leaning against his car like a bored taxi driver, I tried to focus on the things I hated about him and so bury the embarrassed awareness that at least part of me wanted his approval, wanted to be seen to stand up in whatever ways were straight and true.

It was to be the first of several visits I would make to the Interrogation Centre, and at the end of each one I hoped it would be my last. Later on I would read about the imprisoned Nguyen Tai, the most senior North Vietnamese officer ever captured, who after years of physical torture was kept in a sealed white box with twenty-four-hour bright lights and powerful air conditioning turned up high. The memories of my visits stay with me, despite my attempts to shut them away, and flourish into new life with every image of Guantánamo and Abu Ghraib that flickers across my television screen. But it was no one of such high status as Nguyen Tai that Donovan took me to see, even though this captive too was educated and fluent in French. An agent freshly captured in the Cholon district after being recognised in a night market by a defector, and I don't know if it is part of my reluctance to remember but his name is wiped from my memory even though his face is unblurred. He had gone through the inevitable process of denying who he was and hanging on to his assumed identity and carefully constructed background until confronted face to face by some of the very people he had trusted most. I sat in the corner of the room and stared at this first human representative of the enemy we had tried and failed to defeat.

He was probably in his early thirties, wore what looked like home-made rubber sandals, a stained white shirt and black shorts, his hair matted and unkempt – it seemed difficult to associate our military failure with this hunched, forlorn figure. He looked at me once after Donovan had sat down at the table opposite him. I met his eyes and then he looked back to Donovan. What passed between us in that moment? I think of it from time to time and know now that we never saw each other at all but instead saw what the vagaries of fate, which had cast us on a particular side of the line, conditioned us to see, and I do not know if he survived the horrors of that place. If he did, am I even a tiny spot, ingrained in the foulness of his memory? And I do not want to be there in his, or he there in my own, but do not, even all these years later, have the means to erase its existence.

Donovan was quiet, making a play of reading everything in the file before him, barely looking at the man in front of him, sniffing from time to time and then, when he had finished, he leaned back in his chair and smiled. For a second he resembled nothing so much as a doctor with his first patient of the day and, as if to accentuate that impression, there was an air of beneficence about him, a calm, almost languid body language, and I wondered whether, to obtain whatever it was that he wanted, he might not simply lean across the table and whisper in the prisoner's ear. Instead he made a fuss about having the cuffs removed and then offered him a cigarette. The prisoner refused at first but Donovan persisted until one was taken and a fug of smoke enveloped both their heads.

He claimed to be a farmer recruited only recently and that he was someone who wanted simply to go back to his village and work the land – the thing he supposedly knew best. But his hands didn't look like those of a farmer and when they had searched his home they had found books, including poetry, that were unlikely to be the reading material of the background he claimed. Afterwards Donovan told me he had worked as a teacher in a French Catholic *lycée* in Hue. In another life we would have talked about books and Baudelaire.

It was the first time I had heard Donovan speak French and I tried not to smile as he adopted a pronunciation that made it seem as if he resented the words coming out of his mouth, and his knowledge was pretty basic but I hesitated to supply the words he searched for. He could have used Vietnamese translators, but I knew already he didn't trust them and suspected they passed on intel to other sources, so I was stuck with the job of being his conduit and receptor however much I didn't want to be. Once, in his self-conscious fumbling, he glanced at me but I stared back impassively and then, as if wearied by the effort, he got me to translate for him. I was invited to pull my chair closer to the table and so, if I wished, I could have stretched out and touched my enemy on his hands that were small and thin-fingered. As I looked at them I found it irredeemably strange to think that these same hands would kill me if given the chance and had probably killed or arranged the killing of others. And it was of course naive to be surprised that none of this was evidenced in his face. When he exhaled he angled his head slightly and assumed an air of nonchalance, but it was undermined by the tautness of his shoulders and the tight splay of his left hand on the desk. Donovan never lost his smile as he fed me the questions and listened to the answers, sometimes nodding his head as if to convey his acceptance of them.

The prisoner did what I imagine all prisoners must do in such a situation, persisting in a story that moderated his importance, giving information that was already known and keeping close to whatever his questioner needed to know without the ultimate revelation. So he only knew small things, the part of the whole for which he was responsible, and it would always be someone else, someone more important than him, who knew the real answers to what he was being asked. And all the time Donovan displayed a patience that surprised me as the interrogation journeyed through successive cigarettes and when he answered the questions the prisoner looked at Donovan not me.

I guessed the city was full now of such agents, monitoring troop movements, assessing points of weakness in defences and organising possible resistance for when the time came. I should have felt a sense of power as I delivered the questions or when Donovan urged me to ask him something again, or push him further about the North's intentions in relation to Saigon, but instead I had a consciousness that I probably had more in common with the captive than my compatriot and didn't know whether that made me feel pride or shame. But now I try to find some refuge in that sense of irrelevance, telling myself that I was not much more than a cipher in some transaction conducted to rules over which I had little control. And then Donovan played his ace – a family photograph that had been found hidden inside the jacket cover of a book. A woman holding a baby. I watched him place it carefully in the middle of the table, the image still facing him, and he stared at it as if seeing it for the first time. After about thirty seconds he turned it to face its owner. The prisoner barely glanced at it, as if to do so would see them too dragged into the room. Then I asked a series of seemingly innocent questions – what was his wife's name, what gender was the baby and what age? It didn't take a lie-detector test to know that the responses to these questions were hasty fabrications delivered with a spurious indifference, starting with a denial that they were his family.

'Do you want to see them again?' I asked quietly on Donovan's precise instruction – I had begun to understand the need not to just say the words but to replicate the tone he himself used – to which the prisoner shrugged his shoulders as if to say it was a matter of little importance.

Donovan placed his hand on the photograph so that only its edges were visible and then slid it slowly towards him until it slipped off the edge of the table and out of sight. Then, taking his wallet out of his pocket, he produced the family photograph I had glimpsed once before and eased it to the middle of the table. But the prisoner barely glanced at it before staring into the distance.

'Look at it!' Donovan shouted in French, as if he had taken the cursory glance as a personal insult. Then, as the prisoner obeyed, 'I want to see them again. I want to go home to them.'

There was a pause while he carefully retrieved his photograph and gently slipped it into his wallet and I was no longer sure what was genuine and what was theatrical performance. Then he replaced his photograph with the prisoner's and I asked once more if he wanted to see them again.

'Yes,' he answered, allowing himself to look longer at the photograph but still not dwelling on it and probably cursing his sentimental moment of weakness that had compelled him to bring it with him. Much later I would come to understand that betrayal is always found in the weakness of the heart, the wellspring of longing that can make both the innocent and the fanatic equally vulnerable.

'Well you can,' I told him. 'Help me with what I want and you can see them again. But play games with me and you'll disappear off the face of the earth, your ashes scattered by the wind.'

These were the words I said to him. They weren't my words but they were spoken in my voice. And then I had to ask him if he understood. He nodded, but in the next thirty minutes it didn't seem that Donovan managed to prise out of him anything much more than he had already been given and I could sense his rising frustration in his body language as he pushed his chair back from the table several times or blew little streams of air.

'Tell the son of a bitch I'll be back to see him tomorrow and tell him when he tells me the truth he can have his photograph back, can have his family back,' and before I had finished delivering the translation Donovan was hammering on the locked door, impatient for the guard to open it.

But we didn't go back the following day – 'We'll let him stew a little, think things over,' Donovan later told me. And when, in the silence of the car, I tried to make conversation by asking about his children's ages, his gruff answers indicated that these weren't matters he wanted to talk about. Knowing formally about his family also made it impossible to ask about Tuyen, because I could no longer do so without us both sharing the reality of his infidelity and I was fearful of the repercussions if I was to try. And then, as we drove, I endured a fleeting moment of even greater fear that cast me in a future world where the only words I ever uttered were those dictated by him until our voices merged into one and became the ash blown on the wind he had spoken of. So that night, as I hunkered down in my room, I wrote a long letter home that I knew was not for my family's benefit but to reassure myself that my own voice still existed and was not eternally bound to another's will. I know now, of course, that it's what war does and that being part of a collective committed to a shared predetermined aim obviates the individual, and to think otherwise is foolishness. The logical progression of this is that sometimes the voice speaking for you puts words in your mouth that you don't believe or want to express. It's why, too, we always seek to punish the internal dissenter as ruthlessly as the enemy, the man or woman who insists on the primacy of their own voice. And as I wrote that letter I felt an unfamiliar nostalgia for that small-town world where life trundled on in well-established rhythms and the most dramatic changes were the slow turning of the seasons.

When I had finished, the night was too early for sleep and so I went to look for Corley, but when I knocked on his door there was no reply. I hadn't seen him in the best part of a week. I wondered if he was working somewhere or if he was sitting in the Continental like some spiritualist trying to summon the creative stimulus of

Graham Greene. The apartments were quiet and even Madame Binh was nowhere to be found. Not wanting to go back to the solitariness of my room, I headed down the stairs and went outside where the day's clammy heat still lingered and seemed to cling to my face like a mask. A dog sniffed round the base of the tree in front of our gates and from some bar a street away drifted the sound of music. I had started to become increasingly conscious of personal safety and didn't want to walk far from the security of the apartments. There had been a couple of incidents in the city, mostly in the Cholon district. A week before, a shoe-shine boy, no older than eleven or twelve, had exploded a grenade in a restaurant. And there was something else that had begun to shadow my days in that city and for which I had no name but that would come to be an unwanted companion in all the different places my life would take me to live.

That night I went no further than a walk to the Continental, where life appeared to continue undisturbed, and it was there coming out of the entrance that I encountered Corley. Even before he was close enough to speak to me in slurred speech, it was clear that he was drunk. In his hand was his notebook and he had a pen wedged behind his ear, which didn't make him look rakish so much as a builder about to measure up a job in order to give an estimate.

'You OK?' I asked, simultaneously stretching out a hand to catch him as he lurched sideways.

'I've drunk too much. I'm wasted, Mikey, and everything's fucked. Help me get home.'

He draped his arm across my shoulder and we made an unsteady way back to our apartments. A couple of street urchins tugged at our clothes for money and then scampered round our feet so that we almost tripped, and I had to stop and pay them to go away before we could proceed again. Somehow I managed to stagger him across a busy road as Saigon's crazed welter of motor vehicles, bicycles and motorbikes coursed frantically around us. Two young women walking in the opposite direction put their hands across their mouths to hide their laughter, releasing it only when they had passed. And a cyclo driver offered his services but we were close enough to make it back without his aid and paused only once more for Corley to empty his stomach against the base of the tree where a short while earlier I had seen the dog. I stood a little way off, conscious of our mutual embarrassment, and then helped him to his room under the disapproving eye of Madame Binh who had come out of her apartment to see what the noise was and who shook her head and muttered incomprehensibly under her breath.

When I got him into his room and on to his bed, he asked me not to go. I didn't want to stick around, thinking it best if he got to sleep it off, but when he sat up there was an urgency in his voice as he pleaded with me to stay. He was shaking his head and once he jerked his hand as if there were flies buzzing round him. I got him a drink and he held the glass with two hands like a child frightened he might spill its contents.

'We have to get out of here,' was what he said. 'We have to get out, Mikey.'

'It's OK, Corley,' I told him, thinking that it was still the drink talking. 'It's OK.'

'No, Mikey, it's fucked. It's all fucked.'

'You'll be OK in the morning. You need to sleep now.'

But as I made to go he grasped my sleeve and held it tightly.

'You don't understand, Mikey. You, me, we don't understand anything. We've got to get the hell out of here.'

And then he reached to the side of his bed and handed me his notebook.

'Read it, Mikey. No, not later. Read it now. You have to read it – it's the only thing I've ever written that's true.'

He was so agitated that there was no way to avoid his request and so I sat at the end of the bed and opened the notebook.

They're sending me into the field. Can't understand why I'm getting sent as part of a small team but it's all arranged and I'm supposed to visit some villages recently 'liberated' from the Vietcong. I think the order's a mistake because I don't actually need to see anything anymore to write the stories they want. But they tell me it's part of some program being introduced to create first-hand accounts of the good work we're doing, and the terrible consequences if such places fall into Vietcong hands. I'm supposed to link up with some ARVN infantry platoon in the Delta. We were hitching a lift and given seats in a convoy of three Hueys and two Cobra gunship helicopters heading further north. I was issued with a helmet and a flak jacket. There was some confusion about where the rendezvous was supposed to happen but eventually they set us down close to a village sprawling haphazardly along tiered paddy fields.

A spiral of smoke snakes upwards from it and the first thing I experience when I get out of the Huey is the smell of burning and then there's rapid fire for a few seconds and I think this isn't where I'm supposed to be but already the chopper's lifting off, streaming water and vegetation as its blades churn the air. Crazy shouting, screaming, more gunfire, and I start to think that we have stumbled unwittingly into a firestorm, that the Vietcong are still in the village. That it's a trap, that this is where it's going to end. But then I see a small group of ARVN soldiers hunkered down in a circle but they're not sheltering from incoming fire, instead passing a smoke between them and some have their helmets off. And the firing has stopped so there's a strange silence stretching over everything. They look at us with glazed eyes and one of them says something about us that makes the rest laugh. Just beyond them on a dry-earthed rutted pathway I see the first bodies. An old woman and two children. Two kids not much older than five or six. And I think we've all got there too late to save them and that's when I see more bodies in the ditch – maybe as many as twenty – and it looks as if they've been herded there and slaughtered. Women, old people, children – not once did I see an adult male. Out in the paddy fields there are partially submerged bodies face down in the water with their conical hats floating beside them who look as if they've been killed where they worked, or trying to run away. Further out, close to a trembling bamboo thicket, is a splayed line of bodies cut down as they tried to reach the hiding place it seemed to offer.

At the entrance to the village are dead water buffaloes, their grey flanks pocked with red holes, their open eyes frozen in a blue terror. Soldiers walk past us seemingly indifferent to our presence and what lies all around them. Contorted bodies sprawl in the doorways of the ramshackle houses where fires have been started after they've been plundered of whatever little they held of value. Some of them have their faces shot away. Discarded worthless possessions are strewn everywhere. Little more than rags. We've got there too late to save them – that's what I think, and then suddenly I realize that it isn't the Vietcong who did this but the soldiers who walk slowly past me, dead-eyed, sullen of expression, never meeting my gaze. I see an officer and grab his arm, ask him what happened, and he throws my hand off as he says, 'Bad people, hide Vietcong. Feed them.' Then he walks on as he shouts, 'Bad people,' and spits as if they are a foul taste in his mouth.

These are the people we've come to save and tell about all the good things Uncle Sam is going to do for them. And what we've done is try to bomb them into the Stone Age, taken their daughters …

There was more, much more, but I stopped reading. I looked at him and just for a second it was as if I didn't recognise him.

'What the hell is happening here, Mikey?'

'I don't know, Corley. I don't know.'

'It's bad, Mikey. It's really bad,' he said and then he turned his face to the wall.

There was nothing more I could say so I set the notebook on the small table beside his bed because I didn't want to feel it in my hand any longer than I needed. But he insisted, despite my obvious reluctance, that I took it and so I carried away the one and only thing he had ever written that was true.

'I'll look in on you in the morning,' I told him, wanting to leave, but he didn't answer. Then, as I opened the door, I heard him say, 'Turn out the light.' And I left him there with his face turned to the wall.

Afterwards they made him write a story blaming the Vietcong for the killings.

The things that I had read drifted through my dreams and I woke early from a broken and shallow sleep. I waited an hour before I went to check on him. There was no answer when I knocked on his door and I gently opened it to find him sitting on a chair at the window, the gauze curtains shifting slightly in the breeze so that light brushed his face with changing patterns. The room stank of booze.

'You OK, Corley?' I asked.

'I'm OK, Mikey,' he said, staring into the street, and then after a pause, 'thanks for looking out for me last night.'

I shrugged as if to say it was nothing. Voices and the sound of traffic seeped into the room from down below. Somewhere in the building I could hear Jim Croce's 'Time in a Bottle'. I asked him if he wanted to go out and get some breakfast but he said only if I wanted to watch him being sick again.

When he had finally returned to Saigon he had fallen in with some journalists – the hard-core remnants of those who had attended the official war briefings at the Rex that became known as the Five O'Clock Follies, and who had listened with barely disguised cynicism to what they were told and shared in-jokes. He had tried to tell them of the things he had seen but was informed brusquely that there was no yardage in it. That it was just another sad part of the 'Mere Gook Rule' and even more so because the guilty party was other 'gooks'. Instead they had plied him with drink and he had been happy to go along with it, happy to sink into oblivion. He looked pale, more washed-out than I had ever seen him, and I knew it wasn't only caused by his hangover. And the room itself seemed strangely empty, as if his very presence had reduced it to a void, stirred only by the light currents of air from the open window. I had thought I would give him his book back but I knew then it was kinder to keep it.

I would have stayed longer with him, taken the whole day out if needed, but I was scheduled to return to the Interrogation Centre with Donovan. If I could have thought of a way out of it, I would have played that card. I'd already given it a shot by asking Greenberg to tell Donovan that I was needed for something pressing and he should find someone else, but he had looked at me coldly, told me it was outside his control and then added for good measure, 'You've made your bed, Michael, and now you must lie in it.'

My apprehension wasn't eased by Donovan's sullenness that barely acknowledged my existence and when I trailed after him down dismal corridors I felt like a bellhop, with my temporarily needed skill unwanted and burdensome baggage. He seemed smaller, drawn into himself, his shoulders a tight ridge that strained against his jacket, and his heels smacked and echoed in the narrow maze of passageways that seemed to burrow us deeper into the abyss. The room we were shown into looked the same as the previous one but I wasn't sure whether it just shared the same sense of a confined space where there was nothing unnecessary, nowhere to hide, nowhere to offer a window to the outside, permeated with the smell of drains, of stale sweat and piss that seemed to ooze from the very walls.

We sat at the table in silence and waited and then the door was pushed open and two guards dragged in the prisoner.

As soon as Donovan saw him he jumped up and started shouting, 'Who did this? Which one of you bastards did this?' And as the guards bundled the prisoner into his seat, 'I'm taking this to the highest level. Heads are going to roll for this – you better believe it.' But the guards merely shrugged and lowered their eyes, and as we heard their footsteps in the corridor Donovan eased the prisoner into a more comfortable position then steadied him with a hand on his shoulders.

'Get some water, Mikey, and tell those fuckers I want a doctor sent for or somebody's going to get burnt.'

When I returned Donovan was still standing at the prisoner's side, his hand resting on his shoulder, and then with the tip of a finger he angled the man's head to inspect the damage. One side of his face was a swollen pulp, the eye almost closed and his mouth a bloodstained cicatrix. Taking the glass of water, I saw that the prisoner's hands were also bloodied and they shook so much that Donovan had to hold the bottom of the glass to stop it spilling. The prisoner had never looked at us since coming into the room, and I was grateful. I felt sick, like I couldn't breathe, and I had to stop myself beating on the door and hurrying outside to gulp cleaner air.

'Who did this?' Donovan asked in French, and his voice that was little more than a whisper made him sound like a father talking to his child. But there was no reply and the prisoner's gaze was riveted on the table. He took another sip of the water and his hand was a little steadier. Donovan lit a cigarette and gave it to him and the man touched his face lightly, slowly tracing its contours with the tips of his pulped fingers as if struggling to recognise it as his own.

Then for the first time he looked at us, one of his eyes a distorted purple clot, and I could do nothing but meet his stare. What did I see in it? What I remember now was that I didn't see the anger that I might have expected, so much as shame. I guess shame that someone had done this to his flesh and in so doing had dishonoured him and the essence of who he was. It's what has always been done and what we still do – damage the possession of self, erode every core element that serves to form who we are until all that is left is a husk. Only the strongest can survive, those who despite everything are able to turn torture into confirmation of their moral superiority and embrace martyrdom with an even greater zeal. But in those moments I was grateful for Donovan's solicitude, his expressions of contempt for those who had inflicted the beating. So when he started to talk it was with a promise, a promise that I offered in my voice.

'I can trade you. Trade you for one of ours. I can send you home. Back to your family. I've done it before, can do it again.'

The prisoner took the cigarette out of his mouth and the exhaled smoke seemed to leach from the pores of his broken skin.

'You help me and I'll get you out of here, move you somewhere safe until I organise a trade,' Donovan told him, 'and what you need to tell me means nothing to your people any more because we both know how this is going to end, so there's nothing to be gained by you holding on to what can only bring you great suffering.'

Turning to me, he asked if I had translated his words – he had heard the waver in my voice – and there was suspicion in his eyes for a second as if he thought I might have substituted my words for his. And if I could have used my own words what would I have said except begged him to tell Donovan whatever it was he wanted to know so that all of us could be somewhere other than in this room that was devoid not just of air but any sense of – and I'm struggling for the word but perhaps humanness comes closest to what I mean. Because all three of us were indisputably less than who we were although we may not have fully understood it or grasped either how intimately we were suddenly linked in that reduction. When the prisoner spoke his voice sounded as if it came from somewhere far off and the whispery words seemed almost smothered by the smoke from the cigarette so that I had to lean in close to catch them. And when I translated for Donovan he nodded in a way that suggested what he was hearing confirmed everything he already believed.

When it was over he reached across the table and patted the man's forearm and then gave him what was left of the packet of cigarettes. He leaned back on his chair and then, almost as an afterthought, took the photograph of the man's wife and child, studied it as if he was committing it to memory before placing it in the breast pocket of the prisoner's shirt and patting it gently. As Donovan stood up, the man looked at him and asked when he would get traded. It was the strongest voice he had mustered.

'Soon, very soon,' Donovan answered in French as he signalled to me that we were leaving.

'When?' the man asked again, the bloodied tears at the side of his mouth making it look like that of a battered ventriloquist's dummy.

But Donovan was hammering on the door and didn't reply when the question was asked a third time and I heard myself repeat the first given answer of 'Soon, very soon', and when the door was eventually opened I didn't look back.

Neither of us spoke as we retreated down the corridors and I tried to tell myself that their claustrophobic power was unravelling as each step took us closer to daylight. When eventually we reached outside Donovan paused to light a cigarette then said, 'I don't know about you, Mikey, but I need a drink. Might even tip a few. That place gives me the heebie-jeebies.' And if I didn't know him better I might have thought he shivered a little.

'Should we wait for the doctor?'

'The doctor? There's no doctor coming, Mikey.'

'But you told them to get a doctor.'

'For the optics.'

He started to walk but I didn't follow and instead asked him what he meant. He didn't respond and, as I watched him stride away, I suddenly understood.

'You had him beaten. It was you,' I called after him.

'Those bastards don't know when to stop, that's the problem,' he said, turning to look at me. 'I guess they enjoy it too much. Sometimes a little gentle physical persuasion is needed to tip the scales — just to tip the balance in the right direction. Those goons have no sense of proportion — that's the problem.'

I wanted to tell him he was a bastard, wanted to tell him that I was done with him, but instead I simply shook my head in the only form of defiance I was able to muster.

'Now, Mikey, please don't go all Boy Scout on me. I told you once before: this isn't summer camp. And before you start to make a song and dance out of it, you should remind yourself of what they've done to our people.' He walked towards me and threw the cigarette into the gutter as if it was a distraction. 'Tortured half to death, starved and left to rot in bamboo cages. So please, Mikey, whatever speech you're about to give now, don't make an asshole of yourself and don't give me the benefit of your wisdom because I decided a long time ago you don't know shit about anything.'

He was close to my face but I didn't flinch and the only resistance I felt open to me was to return his stare and not step back or falter. So we stood like that for a few silent seconds and then he spun on his heel and started to walk off to wherever he was going to have his drink. But then he stopped and called back to me, 'You should join the one true faith, Mikey, if you're so squeamish. Light a candle, say a Hail Mary, absolve some of that guilt you cripple yourself with.'

I said nothing and watched him go to whatever bar would best serve his purpose. I didn't have the oblivion of drink or Hail Marys to fall back on, so I simply returned to work and lowered my head to the papers on the desk, and at lunchtime I didn't sit under the garden canopy with Danh and Corrine but continued working, trying not to think of a man who believed he was going to be traded, that he was going home. I never saw him again, don't know what happened to him and whether he ever made it back to his family, but if he did I know that I must exist in his memory, as he does in mine, and both of us must wish it were not so.

After that I fell out of contact with Donovan for a couple of weeks – he didn't request my services and I didn't go looking for him and instead kept my head down and wondered how long it would be before I was ordered home. I did eventually go to Vung Tau, but not in Donovan's car – when I told Corley I wasn't asking for it he managed somehow to inveigle a beat-up Renault whose engine threatened to give up at various stages of the journey and whose shot suspension allowed us to feel every bump and pothole on the road. Setting out, it felt good to sidestep Saigon for a few hours, and I'd had enough of its coffee-coloured river and somehow had started to think that the sea and even swimming in it might offer a restoration, however temporary. But an hour south of the city the sky darkened and it began to rain, really coming down so that the wipers struggled to clear it and I had to concentrate on the driving. Corley sat with his feet on the dash and was uncharacteristically quiet. Since the night he had made me read his book neither of us had mentioned what he had witnessed and I think we both believed to do so would take us places neither of us wanted to be, and from where we might not return. He never spoke about it again in my presence and I supposed he had compartmentalised it, put it in as distant a room as possible and locked the door.

I thought of telling him about Donovan and some of the work I had done for him – in an attempt, I suppose, to shoulder some of what he was feeling – but didn't, not least because I was frightened my revelations might leave me damaged in both our eyes. And as the rain continued to beat against the windshield, I knew that my earlier self-comforting but hopelessly mistaken belief that some-how the existence of a moral code held me at a decent distance from what we had done, and continued to do in this far-off country, could no longer be sustained. As that reality coursed through my consciousness, a constant companion through the rain and miles of flooding road, I wanted to be back wherever I decided home was.

When we finally reached Vung Tau, the rain had stopped but everywhere we saw its effects: a host of potholes brimming with the brightening sky's reflections, and awnings and canopy-covered frontages fat-bellied. All about us water sluiced and dripped, flooding through drains and carrying the street's detritus to some new destination. A large rat scurried across our path, its fur rain-beaded and shiny. Only the suddenly blue sky offered a semblance of a welcome and we stretched our legs, glad to be out of the car's confines. A small farmers' market bunched itself up tight under tarpaulins, and the scrawny hens in bamboo cages stuck their necks through the bars to complain to us as we passed. Some kids splashed each other in puddles, high-kicking spray until rebuked by a passing adult. The curved rim of beach was deserted and the sea itself looked calm, almost motionless. I had assumed Corley had been there before, but it turned out he hadn't, and I soon discovered his knowledge of the place was based on the stories he had heard when it was the centre for our troops' R&R. But whatever buzz it once held had long since departed, so what we found was lots of boarded-up dance halls and bars with curiously romantic names or echoes of home. It felt like a ghost town alive only in the memories of the thousands of Americans and Australians who had used it to temporarily escape the conflict. There were a few bars along the front still in business, their customers mostly locals with a sprinkling of Americans, probably employed by the host of private companies who still hoped to make a buck out of development or continued lucratively servicing some part of the military's ongoing needs. But we had come too late for the party.

One open-fronted bar had music coming from it and we stopped there for a drink and watched three musicians — a guitarist–singer, a drummer and a keyboard player all with tinny little instruments — try to replicate pop tunes they had heard on the radio. We played a game of seeing who was first to recognise the song. When we asked the owner if they served food he shook his head but changed his mind and eventually brought us a simple dish of pork and rice. It started to rain again and we moved further inside so that we were close to the tiny stage. I turned to watch the downpour dancing on the plastic tables outside and the scurry of people for shelter, their heads covered with all sorts of improvised protection. The rain darkened the sky and rendered the sea monochrome. A wind started up, fretting the palm trees and scudding up waves in a sea that had suddenly quickened into fierce motion. Then a young woman in a sparkly bikini, white knee-length boots and a cowboy hat came onstage and took over the singing. A huddle of Americans slapped their table until the glasses bounced and rattled as she sang 'Rock Your Baby' and shimmied from side to side then ventured into the audience, teasing and flirting with them but evading their outstretched hands. A couple of them tried to entice her closer with dollar bills but she somehow managed to extract their money without entering their grasp. Corley looked at me and rolled his eyes but we didn't leave and told ourselves it was because of the rain.

Later we walked on the beach. The rain had stopped and the sky was blue once again, as if the previous rain and wind had been just a passing fit of temper, and with some sense of equilibrium restored we took off our shoes and walked along the water's edge. Corley talked of his childhood holidays on the Connecticut coast, the cottage they hired every year and the fishing trips he went on with his father. I had no such childhood memories to offer in return and so I assumed my customary role of listener. We had brought swimming trunks but the sight of raw sewage in the water put an end to that idea and we slipped our shoes on again. As we walked we met two Americans. One of them knew Corley and they stopped to talk for a while. Afterwards he told me that they worked for DAO and were part of a team sent to reconnoitre the area and assess if it would prove a suitable place to ensure a safe evacuation if it was needed. In the event it would never be used but instead in the years after Saigon's fall become the starting point for many of those who sought to escape the new republic. They would set off in small craft and fishing boats under the gaze of the giant Christ who stood high on the hill with his arms outstretched. And I wonder if any of those looking at it thought those outstretched arms were a farewell blessing or a calling back from all the dangers that awaited them.

The trip had been a failure, although neither of us admitted it to the other, and so we told ourselves it made sense to head back before it got dark. Corley drove this time and I mistakenly thought that the concentration this required might stem some of his conversation. But it was only after about an hour of small talk that he fell silent and probably then because I pretended to be asleep. The silence was short-lived.

'Mikey, Mikey,' he said, poking me, and then when I sat up and had given him my attention, 'have you ever done something really stupid?'

I could have given him a long list beginning with our trip to Vung Tau but there was something uncharacteristically tentative about his voice that stopped me falling into facetiousness.

'Yeah, I guess. Lots of things,' I said, but I somehow knew that he didn't mean what Donovan would have described as little chickenshit things and, when he didn't answer right away but firmed his hands on the wheel and stared intently at the road ahead, I knew something out of the usual was coming. And as it wasn't my stupidity he was interested in, I didn't offer to elaborate.

'I trust you, Mikey. There's no one else I can tell and I need to tell someone.'

And just for one crazy and mistaken moment I thought he was going to say, 'You're worth the whole damn bunch put together,' but instead he glanced at me either to visually confirm his evaluation or check that I was really listening.

It made me nervous, and I suddenly didn't want to be the only person in the world he could trust and was no longer sure I was that entirely trustworthy person, so I said, 'You don't need to tell me, Corley. Sometimes it's maybe better to keep stupid things private and after a while they probably don't seem as bad as you think.'

He shook his head in a rebuttal of my words. I turned away from his intensity to stare at flooded fields where peasants worked with water buffaloes in tableaux little changed from bygone centuries.

'I have to tell someone, Mikey, because it's driving me crazy. That night I got drunk ... ' He paused as we squeezed a path between a broken-down truck and an oncoming farmer's cart piled high with some indeterminate crop, then wiped the back of his hand across his mouth. 'That night before I got drunk I went downtown and did the business.'

'You had sex?' I asked, surprised but for some reason not shocked, and trying to evaluate the significance of his disclosure.

'Yes, I had sex.'

'And you feel guilty now. About Sylvia,' I said, hoping that stating the obvious might give me a little time to work out what I should say to him.

'I've cheated on her, Mikey. Cheated on the girl I love with a Saigon bar girl.'

'She doesn't need to know,' I heard myself say, suddenly lapsing into how I imagined someone else might have spoken because I still didn't know the right way to respond.

'But I know. What was I thinking? How am I going to look her in the eye?'

I had no answers to these questions, nor was I able to tell him that I felt he had cheated on me too by leaving me in a club of one. I listened to him say 'shit' over and over again, his blond fringe bouncing with the synchronised jerk of his head. A tiny spot of spit hit the windshield.

'You're in a faraway country doing a difficult job. Under pressure. You'd seen things – bad things. And she hasn't been writing so often as she used to and for all you know she's found someone else.'

'Jeez, Mikey, is that supposed to make me feel better?'

I half-apologised and then stopped myself asking questions about his encounter because I wasn't sure I could hide the fact that they were motivated by curiosity slightly more than concern. And although I felt sorry for his present misery I was also conscious that no particular emotional state seemed to last very long and was as likely to be replaced rather than replenished by time's passage.

94

'How am I going to tell her?'

'Perhaps you shouldn't.'

'I want her to be my wife, so what way is that to start a marriage?'

I was hardly the best person to give him advice, but he had pushed me into that situation and I felt a responsibility of sorts to him, at least in the short term, to help him shed some of his misery.

'It was a mistake, Corley. You regret it deeply and are obviously suffering for it. Why cause her pain as well? You've a whole lifetime to make it up to her.'

'You really think so?'

'I didn't know what I thought, other than we were in a place that had different value systems and different interpretations of truth, and for a second I wondered if it might be possible for your view to be dependent on circumstances and in which world you found yourself. But the dubious complexity of that was too much to unravel and so I simply told him that I did. And as we temporarily slowed in traffic he seemed calmer.

'You're a good friend, Mikey,' he said, dismissing my assertion that I hadn't really done very much.

Then, having donned the mantle not just of loyal friend but of someone suddenly imbued with worldly wisdom, I tried to suggest more consolation by offering, 'And maybe too, however much you regret it and wouldn't ever want to repeat it, it's experience, water in the well. What you were talking about.'

He nodded his head but I could see he wasn't sure and, thinking it best not to venture further into areas where I had so little experience, I retreated into silence as we returned to Saigon.

On that evening neither of us knew how close we were to the end, or how quickly it would come, and I was aware that, despite Donovan's and others' best efforts, there was still a strong school of thought that estimated Saigon could be held until at least the following year, while Martin and to a lesser extent Polgar persisted in their belief that some negotiated settlement could be reached. But because the Peace Accords had proved nothing more than worthless paper, each waking moment was now filled with an apprehension of what was about to happen. In my apartment the martial music being played in Lam Son Square sounded ever more strident and there were night-time warnings from loudspeakers mounted on military vehicles that the curfew was about to begin. Despite the security cordon thrown around the city, it was too late to stop the deluge and soon Saigon was overflowing as more and more refugees flooded in, their ranks swollen no doubt by both army deserters and enemy agents. It was a city bulging at its already crowded seams and in a constant state of flux that threatened to tumble into unmitigated chaos. And everything was for sale, everything had a price, as fear-driven commerce flourished on every street and in every level of society without restraint. Family groups containing young children and elderly parents traversed the city, seemingly carrying everything they owned. Where they were heading was a mystery. And if a smaller number of bar girls still touted for business, most of them had abandoned the garish costumes that proclaimed their trade, while the ARVN soldiers who roamed the streets shouldering weapons looked permanently high and gave the impression they were ready to turn them on anyone who got in their way.

I hadn't seen Donovan for a while, but, just when I thought he might have dispensed with my services or become too heavily focused on the growing crisis, he reappeared in our offices, something he had never done before, sniffing as he looked around, studying Corrine longer than was polite and speaking to me as if nothing had happened between us.

'Good to see you, Mikey. Still shuffling paper? You're going to have to leave it for a while because I need you to help me win the war.' And, turning to Corrine, he said, 'You mightn't know it, but Mikey is Uncle Sam's secret weapon.'

She smiled out of her unfailing politeness and lowered her head to her work, but I was conscious that others were looking at us and, reluctant as I was to spend more time with him, I didn't want to be embarrassed in front of people I considered my friends, so I secured my desk and found him outside joshing with the guards and handing out cigarettes.

'Have you got a jacket?' he asked, and when I told him it was back at the apartment he drove me over to get it, explaining that we were meeting some important people and needed to look sharp. When we got there he followed me in, taking Madame Binh's hand, kissing it and, to her obvious pleasure, telling her that his heart had never left. Then, as I unlocked my door, he told me his first billet had been the room at the end of the same corridor. I expected him to wait but he followed me and I saw him taking everything in, even running his finger across the spines of my books and angling his head to read the titles. I didn't want him to touch them. Wanted them to be at the heart of what separated him from me. When I put on my jacket he brushed a bit of fluff from my shoulder and straightened my collar.

'Do I need a necktie?' I asked, trying to sound just the right side of sarcastic.

He shook his head and then, with a final glance round the room, went back out to the car. But he didn't start the engine and, turning himself sideways, began to explain.

'You probably know from the reports that flow across your desk about what happened in Danang, but in case you don't, it went down like a house of cards and there was nothing but chaos – bloody chaos and a lot of things left behind, good people too, left to fend for themselves, and the ARVN trampling anything in their way to be on the boats or planes and save their own necks. People clinging to the wings and landing gear of planes, people drowning in the sea in a stampede to get on a boat. And, Mikey, as God is my witness, that's what's going to happen right here in Saigon unless we kick things into faster motion, stop trusting in some Hail Mary pass that Charlie's going to sign up to a beautifully civilised negotiated settlement. If we can't make those in charge here understand that, we've got to go round them, do whatever needs to be done until someone listens. You understand?'

I told him I did, all the time wondering who we were going to meet, and when I asked he said, 'There's a small group of big shots on an important Senate Select Committee who've come to see for themselves, and we need to make sure they take the right messages back to Washington, not the bullshit they're being fed out of the Embassy.'

'And where do I come into this?'

'Just be the Ivy League boy, Mikey, the educated languages expert, and if I call on you tell them about all the interviews we've done with reliable – no, impeccable sources – who've told us that the North isn't interested in anything other than a complete military victory. And tell them that they're preparing for a final all-out push, that they're going to be outside our gates pretty damn soon.'

'Do I make some of it up?' I asked.

'Do whatever you need to do.'

'What if they ask questions?'

'Use your imagination, Mikey – all those books you read must be dripping with it – and I'll be there to bail you out if needed.'

We drove slowly across the congested city, where every street was choked with traffic and accompanied by an incessant and frustrated blare of angry horns through which we made our own expletive-laden snail trail, Donovan's increasingly strident curses adding to the unrelenting din. The location for the meeting was in a safe house, a private villa in a wealthy district with tree-lined boulevards where the French had lived out their dream of empire. We passed through the metal gates and some security, then into the villa itself. My first impression was of air-conditioned opulence. Five Americans, in crumpled lightweight suits that suggested they weren't long off a plane, sat on black leather settees round a coffee table drinking coffee and Jack Daniel's. A woman wearing a dark suit and a pearl necklace sat to one side with an open notebook and pen poised to take dictation and looked as if she had stepped straight out of a Washington office. There was another American standing behind them with a glass in his hand. I saw him look at his watch and shake his head at Donovan before describing him as one of our most valued analysts.

'Gentlemen, apologies for our lateness – an urgent situation detained us,' Donovan said in reply and then he introduced me as 'an experienced field officer, a linguistics expert, who had conducted extensive interviews in both French and Vietnamese with a number of our best sources'.

I simply nodded and hoped I looked vaguely like the person he had described. The woman started taking notes but Donovan intervened, telling the gathering that, due to the extreme secrecy of the intelligence he was about to share, he didn't want it minuted or attributed to a specific individual. After some brief discussion his wish was granted and when the secretary left the room he started to give a detailed reading of the situation, referring to interviews and occasionally glancing at his pocketbook when he was itemising dates or supposedly quoting some source.

'Let me get this right,' one of the senators interrupted, 'the South Vietnamese army is liable to crumble once the attacks start. Is that what you're saying?'

'Yes, sir,' Donovan replied. 'Our best intelligence is that morale is mostly shot to pieces. And we have reports already of desertions and some of the commanders organising their departures and those of their families.'

'Despite all the money and equipment that's been pumped in?' another asked.

'Yes, sir.'

'That's not what we're getting out of the Embassy.'

'No disrespect to the Embassy, but I'm outlining our findings as openly and as honestly as possible and without prejudice. I think Mr Bloomfield's intelligence sources are corroborating what we believe to be the reality of the situation,' Donovan said as he held a hand out to the standing American in a gesture of invitation.

So this was George Bloomfield, the seeming object of Donovan's implacable enmity. I didn't understand and, as Bloomfield accepted the opportunity to give his support to the analysis just delivered, I looked at this slightly overweight man a few years older than Donovan who was clearly sweating despite the air conditioning. He wore large heavy glasses that made his eyes look as if they were peering out from under rippled water and from time to time he pushed them back on the bridge of his nose with a finger. I don't know exactly what I had expected but I guess it would have been someone more obviously combative, someone cut from similarly aggressive cloth as Donovan.

'All our sources are telling us similar things to what you've just heard. I believe Mr Donovan's analysis is wholly correct.'

'So why are we hearing from Ambassador Martin this very morning that he retains his confidence in the South Vietnamese and that Saigon is safe for the foreseeable future?'

'I guess he's reluctant to panic anyone unnecessarily,' Donovan said, shrugging his shoulders as if to say please don't ask me to call the Ambassador a schmuck. 'But listen to what Mr Miller has to say, based on the extensive interviews he's conducted with our own agents, well-placed defectors and captured enemy.'

They all stared at me, no one more intently than Bloomfield, and after a moment's hesitation I told them what Donovan wanted. There were no immediate questions, just a row of nodding heads, and after I had finished Donovan ushered me off the scene to wait for him in the car, either to avoid the possibility of subsequent ones or because he didn't want me to hear any more of what was being said. When eventually he came out I didn't ask him how it had gone.

'Went pretty well, Mikey,' he said as if I had, 'but these fact-finding trips are a dime a dozen. They get a bit of wining and dining and hear only what someone needs them to hear. And they never go off track or step outside the carefully prepared schedule that's been arranged for them – probably the political equivalent of flower arranging or a puppet show. These guys, however, are heavyweights and when they go back they'll squawk in the right ears and to their contacts in the press.'

'And Bloomfield?'

'What about him?'

'You're working together?'

'We couldn't have got them there without his say-so. They're supposed to be somewhere else right now.'

'But Bloomfield ... you hate him.'

'This isn't the schoolyard, Mikey. When he's right he's right, whoever he is, and he's right when he's seeing what's as plain as the nose on the end of your face.'

So Donovan and Bloomfield had made a truce for the greater good. It was just another turn of that bewildering merry-go-round of alliances and internecine power struggles that I couldn't even begin to grasp. And when I think back now, there were always parts of the picture missing so it meant I never had access to a fuller understanding and had to interpret both people and events from that limited perspective, often relying on little more than instinct. As we headed back towards the Embassy, Donovan stressed the need for the meeting to be completely confidential and once again I found myself to be the possessor of a particular secret and didn't know whether it was a good one or something that might be better shared.

A few days later, just after I had arrived at work, Donovan appeared again, rubbing sleep out of his eyes, and his clothes looking like he had slept in them. But he hardly had time to speak when there was the sound of gunfire and a massive explosion that rattled the building. My first thoughts were that we were under attack, but when I went to the window I saw the guards pointing skywards. Donovan meanwhile had spun on his heels and was hurrying out to the stairs, as he ran telling people to stay away from the windows. On impulse I followed him up the stairs and out on to the building's roof. I heard the wheezing approach of Greenberg and we both looked as Donovan pointed to where a jet was speeding away. There was a rising plume of black smoke. Car horns shrieked and dogs barked in a crazy crescendo.

'It must have hit the Embassy,' Donovan said.

'I think it's the presidential palace,' Greenberg said, still breathless and pointing in the direction of the smoke.

'I think you're right,' Donovan told him and we all stared across the roofs and wondered what it meant.

Later, we learned that no one had been killed and that the pilot was trained by us but, despite the limited physical impact, psychologically it erased any lingering fantasy of the city as a protected enclave and set everyone on edge. It was a feeling that was soon accentuated by the sound of approaching warfare. Eventually Xuan Loc, the last defensive line between the enemy and Saigon, would collapse. But before that happened there would be other people on that same roof, and other roofs throughout the city, in the shape of DAO construction teams frantically clearing spaces where small UH-1 helicopters might safely land. The black flights out were already underway and amongst a panicked population, a panic that we had helped to create, rumour and counter-rumour coursed like electricity through the streets. The martial music in Lam Son Square was momentarily replaced one night just before midnight by the scream of warning sirens and the sibilant hiss of incoming rocket fire.

Everything now blurs in its precise chronological sequence as I remember how things rushed to their inevitable end and the city became the eye of the storm, its streets filling with a panicked population, a continued influx of refugees and sullen soldiers carrying their M16s like curses ready to explode. Non-essentials were being shipped out in chartered and scheduled flights and in C-141 transports. I couldn't decide whether I had become an essential or whether I had been simply forgotten about, but no one made any attempt to inform me or allocate a departing flight. Corley left at short notice, being given a seat on a plane to Thailand when someone declined it at the last moment. I knew because I found a note slipped under my door when I returned later the same day. Long lines formed outside the Embassy, ever-increasing sums of money changed hands for exit visas or a set of forged papers, and some of those elegant houses in the rich boulevards were being sold for a fraction of their former value or hastily boarded-up. Businessmen everywhere tried to decide whether to stay or go and the evacuation of Vietnamese that was well intentioned and ultimately facilitated by many brave people was tainted by the places won by self-interest and personal loyalties, rather than the priority of need.

All of those Vietnamese I worked with were 'endangered' but they still turned up every day and did whatever tasks reached their desks. Then, one afternoon after the doors had been closed and all non-essential staff cleared from the building, Greenberg addressed them and promised everyone safe passage out as soon as it was necessary, even offering, if slightly vague, assurances about immediate family members. Soon after, though, he too was gone – I learned later that he had taken his cook and maid with him. Some of the staff began bringing suitcases to work and a group started to sleep in the building, so that in the morning the office was filled with the smell of the previous evening's food. Gradually the flow of work petered out and on the rare occasions a courier arrived he would find himself stared at intently before they realised he had not come with the news they were waiting for. In the absence of incoming work the translators would huddle in small groups and sometimes voices were raised. Inevitably I became the focus for their questions and I felt their increasing frustration with my lack of information and sensed that some had started to suspect I was withholding what I knew from them. They discreetly watched me, and that included Danh and Corrine, perhaps looking for some sign, hoping to detect some glimmer of knowledge, and even when I went to the washroom I felt their eyes following me as if they were uncertain as to whether I would return. I put on an act of being relaxed but repeatedly phoned people in the Embassy, to be told each time that everything was under control and an inventory of staff had already been made, that arrangements were being put in place and that in the meantime it was vital to avoid any kind of panic. All my attempts to contact Donovan ended in failure and no one seemed able to put me in touch with him. I began to believe that, like Greenberg, he too had left.

After receiving a directive we had started to burn documents – and that, of course, told its own story to my colleagues. Each day I felt a tightening pressure in my chest, an ever-growing weight of anxiety that spilled over into fear. It was intensified by my sense of isolation and an apprehension that I too might be abandoned. When Embassy staff did come, it was only to arrange for the removal of the remaining files and soon they were being driven away in makeshift crates, no doubt to a quicker and more reliable destruction. One of the staff involved was the security officer who had removed Corley from the Ambassador's lawn, but when I tried to elicit information from him he merely shrugged and told me I needed to speak to someone higher up the food chain.

Things started to fall apart completely. One afternoon as I sat at my desk I was conscious of something stirring. There was an unnatural silence for a few minutes and then a rush of whispering that grew gradually into shouting. People stood up, a chair was overturned and paper fanned out from a desk in a fall to the floor. A growing group had gathered at the end of the room and raised voices were arguing. There was some pushing and then people trying to restrain one individual, trying to calm him before he frantically broke free, and soon he was coming towards me. He was one of the languid badminton players whose face was now contorted with anger. The rest of the office trailed in his wake and more chairs got knocked over. I stood up to ready myself for whatever was coming and he lunged at my desk, banging on it with two clenched fists, but made no attempt to touch me. Words poured out of him in broken English, not all of it making sense but the meaning perfectly clear. They were all going to end up with their throats cut, guns put to their heads. They were good as dead. Why had no one come for them when whores and thieves were getting flown out? Every day more and more. The rest of the office workers grouped behind him, ready to physically restrain him if needed but wanting the same answers as he did. They had worked for us, he shouted, and now they were being betrayed. Left to die, their families left to rot. The Northern troops were closer every day to Saigon. Their rockets were already falling in parts of the city. When I looked over his shoulder I saw Corrine and others crying.

He paused momentarily, exhausted by his passion, and then other voices took his place. When would the Americans come for them? Promises had been made. Greenberg had lied. He had gone. Everyone was lying to them. Everyone was going. People who had given no service were getting seats on planes. Whole families of the worst kind. Visas and seats were being sold. Who could they trust any more? I had no ready answers and I knew that platitudes and phoney assurances were not going to cut it. With the rising hysteria I felt a sense of danger. Some of the faces staring at me looked close to breaking point.

'I'm still here,' I said. 'I'm still here.'

It was all I could think to say but I knew it wasn't enough to mollify them.

'You too will go,' a voice shouted from the back of the crowd.

Someone said that he would kill himself rather than fall into the hands of the Vietcong. Others shouted about the years of service they had given and that they were known to work for the Americans, that their names and their family names were known. There was nowhere for them to hide. They needed to be flown out.

I told them an inventory had been made, that the Embassy had promised to get them out and that all of them were on the official list of those endangered, but it did little to quell their fears. Greenberg's desertion had helped destroy the credibility of such promises. And they gauged rightly that I wasn't someone of enough standing to guarantee them anything. So, faced with someone they knew couldn't give them the needed answers, gradually their anger spent itself and instead was replaced by an almost tangible sense of despair. If anything, this was even worse and, as I watched them slowly walk away and huddle once more in corners, I resolved again to do whatever I could to ensure their safety.

It would be the last time I visited the Embassy, its gates now locked and guarded by Marines, so I had to struggle to gain entry, while all the time beseeching hands pulled at my clothes and people tried to shove letters in front of me, supposedly evidence that they had worked for us in some capacity. Inside was a kind of organised chaos where the central preoccupation appeared to be cremating things. Burnt flakes of paper drifted like black snow from every rooftop incinerator that could be fired, while in every office shredders churned our dying empire of paper into confetti until the hysterical machines overheated.

I struggled to locate anyone willing to admit responsibility, but after being passed from person to person I eventually found someone, who found someone else in a half-abandoned office where the phones screamed constantly until staff lifted them off their hooks, and who told me that things were in hand. That I was to be assured things would be taken care of. I probably felt the same level of confidence in this assertion that my colleagues had when they listened to my faltering attempts at reassurance. But there was nothing more I could do, and although I also made enquiries about Donovan, no one seemed to know anything of his whereabouts or be willing to share their knowledge if they did. When I was leaving I passed an office where, through a partially open door, I saw a woman sitting at a typewriter and silently crying, her glasses pushed high on her head. I walked on and out again into the same drift of black snow.

It's not possible to talk about that time without history attempting to take ownership of your story and what you want to recount risks being replaced by the images that it has imposed on it – the ant line on top of the apartment building climbing into the helicopter; the frantic crowds being repelled as they try to get into the Embassy; the South Vietnamese helicopters pushed off the aircraft carriers into the South China Sea to make room for the next arrivals. All of these clamour for precedence but I didn't see these things, although their frequent repetition on-screen sometimes makes me think that I must have. However, there are other insistent memories I hold and which refuse to be permanently pushed aside.

When I returned to my apartment in a block that already felt eerie in its semi-emptiness, I discovered I had a visitor. Madame Binh, who clearly possessed a key I wasn't aware of, had let her in and she sat straight-backed on my bedside chair. It was Quyen. I had never seen her anywhere other than La Porte Bleue and I mumbled something in confusion. She had been smoking while she awaited my arrival and it shrouded her in a hazy gauze that, coupled with her dark clothes, made her look spectral. She stood up and gave a little bow of the head before brushing ash from her sleeve, but she didn't speak and I couldn't think of the right phrase that would allow her to explain why she was there, so to break the stretching silence I offered tea which she quietly declined and when I gestured to her she sat down again.

'I do not come for myself,' she said, after another pause and without the need for preamble. 'It is too late for us. Vien will never leave, no matter what happens. His family means too much to him. He has always provided for them. And I will never go if he stays, even though he begs me to.'

I simply nodded while frantically trying to anticipate what she was going to say.

'It is for Tuyen that I come to ask.'

'Tuyen?'

'Yes. She must get out. Leave before it is too late.'

'Surely Donovan is the man to ask. He will look after all of you – you have helped him. He knows the people who can arrange things. They have to look after you.'

'We have not heard from Donovan. He doesn't take our calls any more. Do you know where he is?'

I shook my head and I could see her welling up, but she had too much pride to cry in front of me and she blinked it away then briefly looked at the floor before returning her gaze.

'We do not trust him any more. We have nothing more to give him so maybe we are no more use to him.'

I heard myself about to utter some comforting rebuttal of what she had said, but knew the time for lies had gone.

'I haven't heard from him,' I told her, 'and I don't know where he is but I'll go to the Embassy in the morning and try to sort things for all of you.'

'It is no use,' she said, shaking her head. 'He has too many friends. They will not help us leave. You are the only one who can help Tuyen now.'

'Why will they not help you leave?'

'Because of Tuyen. Because of Donovan.'

'I don't understand.'

'He doesn't want her in America,' she said, and then I guess in response to my look of incomprehension and only after her obvious hesitation, 'Tuyen is pregnant with his child.'

I sat on the edge of the bed, trying to take in everything she had said, but all of it slowly made sense. The only thing that didn't was why she had come to me and what was the help only I could give.

'You are the only one who can help her now,' she said again, but I still didn't understand. 'You can take Tuyen with you. You can say you are getting married. That she is having your child.'

She stood up and her eyes were pleading. From outside in the street came a stutter of distant gunfire. We both looked to the window.

'We can pay you,' she said. 'We have dollars. And Tuyen make a good wife. Very good wife.'

'It's not about money. I don't want your money,' I told her as I tried to think what to say.

And what thoughts rushed through me in those moments? Tuyen's beauty, undoubtedly – I couldn't look at her mother without being reminded of that – but so many other things as well. There was the sense that they were owed and the opportunity to repay some of that debt had fallen to me. In some way it felt like the honourable thing. So I could do what they asked but I knew too my responsibility to Tuyen and her child wouldn't stop at a seat in a plane, even if I could engineer it, and a little part of me had already started to think that Donovan might be willing to see me conveniently forgotten about – just another administrative oversight in the chaos of war. It was paranoia, of course. But there were other questions seeking answers. Abandoning her in a strange land was little different in my thinking to abandoning her in Saigon. But how could I make such a commitment to someone who had taken so little notice of my presence and in the normal course of events would never seek to be part of my life? And more than these, and shadowing everything else, was my instinctive aversion to becoming in an instant the surrogate father of Donovan's child. The child – I always imagined him as a boy pressed in the mould of his father – was destined to be a constant reminder of what I wanted to forget and a lasting impediment to everything I longed for. Quyen saw my hesitation and took a step closer. Her hand reached out to my arm.

'I think you are a good man,' she said and she was welling up again. 'Please do this for Tuyen.'

But the good man she saw was already beginning to think of escape routes, of imagined wives, invented fiancées – for some reason the archaic word 'betrothal' ricocheted round my brain. It felt like too much was being asked and ran counter to all the dreams I held about love, and yet another voice told me it was a simple and decent action that might serve to redeem a little of what we had done that was wrong.

'I should try to get her out, get all of you out through the Embassy,' I told her, momentarily avoiding the need for a decision.

'He won't let that happen,' she said. 'I know he won't.'

'I'll find other people. People who will listen. I'll come in the morning. I promise.'

She took a fat envelope from her pocket and held it out to me but I refused, telling her that I didn't want her money and again that I would come in the morning. But the words offered her little comfort and she hesitated and, suddenly sensing for one terrible second that she was thinking of offering herself and desperate to avoid that mutual humiliation, I raised my hands and told her that I was going to do everything possible to help. That she could trust me. Then, bowing her head, she was gone and I stood at the window and watched her cross the street below until her lingering scent and the smoke of her cigarette were the only evidence of her presence.

In her absence I tried to make a decision. I knew Donovan wasn't good at sharing things with most people in the Embassy, particularly in relation to sources, and for all I knew Vien, Quyen and Tuyen weren't on anyone's radar except his own. And why hadn't I been shipped out? I couldn't imagine that anyone thought of me as essential. So several conflicted hours after Quyen left my room I made my decision, and I would be less than honest if I didn't admit that, in addition to whatever redemptive element there might have been, it also involved the configuration of two very contrasting impulses. However unworthy it might sound now, a part of me at least saw it as allowing me to exert retribution on Donovan, while another, very different part imagined it as the romantic gesture that my life had never been given the opportunity to make. So yes, I would offer Tuyen my protection, claim her to be my prospective wife, and let the future take whatever course fate decreed.

The streets were crowded and frenetic in the hours before curfew and the air felt brittle with apprehension and menace before being suddenly riven by thunder. While I searched for a taxi I saw a fist fight between a group of young men disputing the ownership of a Honda while military jeeps passed by indifferently. Ragged families carried what looked like the totality of their possessions on their backs and in small carts but I had no idea where they were heading. Some of the sidewalks had been transformed into impromptu shopfronts selling everything from refrigerators to what looked like surplus ARVN gear. When I eventually got a taxi the driver was intensely silent and I was conscious of his resentful eyes glancing at me at intervals in his mirror. He turned down a couple of streets I wasn't familiar with and for a few seconds I wondered where he was taking me. After I repeated the name of my destination he merely flicked his head slightly then mumbled something under his breath. But eventually we pushed out into an almost solid block of traffic running parallel with the river and, realising it would be quicker to walk, I got him to pull over.

Even the river seemed consumed by people trying to escape, and all sorts of small craft competed for clear water, flitting round the larger vessels like tiny fish. There was more thunder and people stopped in the street and looked upward, unsure if what they heard was man-made.

On some rotting, buckling jetties stretched lines of people awaiting passage or loading every type of domestic and human baggage into whatever vessel their money could buy. From time to time a brief burst of small-arms fire would ignite and then fall silent as if some argument had been settled or been deemed unworthy of continuing. I could see La Porte Bleue in the distance but as I got closer I realised that its window was dark and the outside tables and chairs were empty. The front door was closed but not locked and when I entered I found the inside lit only by what light filtered from the hallway and shadowed my movements. I called out but there was no reply and, as I approached the back room where I had sat so often with Donovan, I half-expected to see him at a table with one of his agents or swigging a beer with Vien. But the room was empty and my footsteps echoed in the silence and I started once when my foot kicked a fallen ashtray and sent it skimming under tables. I opened the door, the one through which I had first seen Tuyen emerge, and called again but there was no response. Finding myself in the back hallway, I opened the doors that led off it, to discover only empty rooms. One of them was clearly Tuyen's and I lingered long enough to lightly touch some of the objects on her bedside and dressing table, but of her or her parents there was no trace. I wondered if Donovan had made arrangements for them, and whether even then they were flying to safety, and I was a little regretful that they would never know that I had come to do the right thing and that I was no longer able to make perhaps the only romantic gesture that life might offer me.

There was someone in the restaurant. A table or chair rattled as if someone had brushed it in passing. I called out, but the sound of my voice was met only by whispers followed by silence and then, when I retraced my steps to the front room, I found myself looking at two men. The one who had gone behind the counter was holding a wooden truncheon and when he saw me his companion pulled a knife from the waistband of his trousers. They shouted at each other and then at me – speaking too quickly for me to understand but I needed no translation to know that I was in danger. Were they Vietcong looking for an early revenge on those who in their eyes had collaborated with the enemy, or merely looters? I held up both my hands in a submissive gesture and the smaller of the two men raised his knife and pointed it. He was wild-eyed, shouting and pointing with the knife, and at first I didn't understand before realising he was gesturing to my watch, allowing me to hope that my fate might be to be mugged rather than murdered. I handed it over and, after pocketing it, he gestured once more and I knew he wanted my wallet. When I started to reach inside my jacket he began screaming, probably fearful that I was pulling a gun, and he jabbed closer to me with the blade.

But the hand that held the gun belonged to Donovan and the voice shouting was his voice. The two men stared at him, and for a second I thought the one threatening me with the knife was about to take me as a shield, but on Donovan's order I moved quickly away and took my place at his side. He gestured them to drop their weapons and again on his instruction I picked up the knife.

'Where's Vien and Quyen? And Tuyen – where are they?' he asked, not taking his eyes off the two men.

'They're not here. I don't know where they are.'

'Are you sure? Have you looked in the back?'

I told him I had, but knew it wasn't good enough for him, and then after he had signalled both of the intruders to lie face down with their hands behind their backs he handed me the gun.

'Shoot the first son of a bitch that moves.'

The butt of the gun bore the sticky warmth of his hand, and I tried to hold it steady as if it was a natural extension of my arm while I listened to the sound of doors opening and banging shut, and I suddenly realised that, despite all my vacillating psychological profiles I had completed, I could shoot someone if I was as frightened as I was in that moment. He was only gone a couple of minutes, but it seemed too long, and when he returned he was shaking his head as if he couldn't believe they had left. After he'd taken the gun off me we both walked to the door and he looked out into the street but signalled me to wait.

'If you'd like your watch back, Mikey, now would be a good time to get it.'

'It's a piece of junk,' I told him, wanting only to be gone.

'When you get outside, turn left and walk to the car. I'll be right behind you, and when you get in you're riding shotgun, so reach for it under the blanket in the back seat and give it plenty of visibility until we're well out of here.'

It was to be his last need for me to 'stand up straight and true'. And as we made our way through the city's streets I stumbled into a thanks, but he told me to 'shut the fuck up' because he had to think and he couldn't do that if I was going to jabber on, so I never told him about what Quyen had wanted of me or offered any explanation as to why I was in La Porte Bleue, and he never asked. Perhaps we both already knew.

It was also the last time I was to see him because, just before dawn the following morning, the few of us remaining in the apartments were loaded on a bus that stopped briefly at other prearranged collection points across the city, then headed for Tan Son Nhut airbase where we sidestepped the mounting chaos of processing to take our seats on an Air America flight. But there was no flight out for Danh and Corrine, the badminton players, or any of my other colleagues. We left them standing in line on a stairwell, their worldly goods stuffed into single suitcases, some of them clutching young children in their arms and all of them waiting for the promised chopper that never came. And as I travelled through a city still opaque despite the first ingress of morning light, I saw my final image of that world slowly emerge – all along the side of the road little pyres of discarded uniforms, helmets and boots, their owners now joining the legions of ghost soldiers, before they too vanished forever.

CROSSING OVER

When my father gathered our family into the basement and led us in the singing of 'Rock of Ages, cleft for me/Let me hide myself in thee', with our wavering voices accompanied by the screaming descant of warning sirens, even as a ten-year-old boy I knew that we were singing to try and stem the fear – the fear that made my mother envelop my younger sister so only her small head was visible as we huddled against the upturned table and mattress I had helped my father drag downstairs. The singing didn't get much past the second verse because, apart from my father, none of us could remember the words and suddenly he decided that there were other things that needed to be done. So despite my mother's pleading he went back up and returned a few minutes later with a box and a sheaf of papers that looked like legal documents of some sort. Already there was the white bounce and drum of giant hailstones against the roof and basement windows. Then again, despite my mother's insistent cautions, he told me to come with him and help carry other stuff into the cellar that I guess he thought was important, and I remember that this unexpected elevation into a kind of manhood briefly surpassed any sense of fear I felt as I followed him up the stairs.

I saw it first. Across the fields. Then he did too and, as if momentarily paralysed, we both stood silent and still, staring at this thing that was coming. It was the closest I have ever felt to him even before his drawn-out end, because it was the only time that all the strengths in which his life of faith wrapped himself fell away, and we stood there side by side, as equals, with nothing separating us in the course of our shared fear.

A blackened world, a sky funnelling and twisting itself in an approaching fury. The row of trees bordering the furthest field suddenly tattered and torn, everything broken-backed and flailing. Black-winged bats of careering debris, the air flecked and scarred, and the roar, the roar louder than anything I have ever heard or want to hear again, like some wild beast tearing itself finally free from a chained torment. The field being ripped up and relaid yard by yard. The hairs of the whole world standing on end.

My father never spoke, never uttered a single word, and then I felt his hand pummelling me back towards the cellar, but as we rushed towards it I carried one final image as the crack of thunder spliced with the slap of our feet on the wooden boards – the churning vertical funnel flaring out like a black sea about to flood over us. I almost fell down the stairs into my mother's outstretched arms and the four of us squeezed into the tightest embrace where it was impossible to tell where one body ended and another began. Even amidst the roar I could hear my mother's breathing and feel the beat of her heart. And then my father was praying that God would protect us and that this thing would pass over us, but before he could finish it hit, and his words were lost in my sister's crying and the small cellar windows smashing open as in it rushed, a hissing blast filling the air with the gathered debris scooped up from the field and a grainy, grit-filled tumulation that tasted like metal in the mouth. Above our heads wood was tearing and screaming and at any moment it felt as if the trembling house might be picked up complete and tossed into the spinning vortex. We buried our faces in each other – it was the physically closest our family had ever been and the strength of my father's arm circled us like a hoop holding us ever tighter. I thought of miracles, of things made right and furies calmed, of men walking through flames, and then it passed, but we didn't move for a long time until slowly and uncertainly we eased apart our still-shaking limbs.

'Is it gone?' my sister asked and my mother kissed her on the head and told her it was.

'Praise God,' my father said but only my mother said amen.

I wanted to be out of the basement, with its acrid, dust-filled air, but my father imposed caution on us and went first. He was gone a few minutes before returning and telling us that we could come out but we were to stay close to him. We had survived but the world we knew had physically changed. A long section of our roof had gone, leaving a gaping tear where my bedroom was, my map of the world somehow still clinging defiantly to a remaining gable and all the house front windows smashed by flying objects. A surf tide of assorted debris had washed up against our walls and yard fencing simply vanished. The house seemed to lean in on itself as if hugging the open wound of the ripped roof. Our neighbours stumbled into the street, some of them rubbing their eyes as if awakened from a deep sleep or because they couldn't trust what they were seeing. Mr Yabowski's car was flipped on its back and their front-yard tree had fallen across the garage, with timber and cladding melding in a broken mess. Down the street a snapped power cable showered blue sparks in a startled quivering fit and everywhere smelt strange as if an electric current had surged through it. My father said 'Praise God' for the second time and urged us to join with him because we were safe.

But I wasn't safe – never throughout the rest of my life was I ever to feel wholly safe. And as I looked up at my father and then at our torn home, I wanted to ask him why he hadn't painted blood on our side posts and on the lintel, why he hadn't done this so God would know we were his and the destroying angel might pass over us.

The years pass, if not with the blink of an eye then certainly with an increasing sense of indecent haste, but the need for a house with strong walls is embedded deep inside me and, when in retirement we came east to live by the coast, I resisted Julia's desire to buy one of the older houses fronting the Atlantic, pointing out all the work that would be required, but not telling her my reluctance was also prompted by my apprehensions about nature unleashed, of rising tides and storms fermenting out at sea before they barrelled towards land. So in the end we bought a place a couple of streets back but close enough to feel the ocean's incessant restlessness sift through the lineaments of our lives, walk the morning shore and, when we watched wind-tossed gulls, know we had the comfort of some-where solid to which we could return.

But a house now with too many empty rooms, and all of them tainted with the slow seep of loneliness. A house that gradually feels as if it's no longer shutting things out so much as shutting them in. Even the furniture that accompanied us in our many different homes, and which we eventually brought from the old world to the new, is marked by the deep patina of memory – a chair found in Portobello Road, a small table bought in a Madrid antique shop, crystal bedside lights Julia discovered in a flea market in Amsterdam. Sometimes, in passing, I let my hand touch them, as if through that brush of my fingers I might be able to rejuvenate the memories I hold of her and our life together.

Let's sketch the details, if only to get them out of the way. I don't want a life story to get in the way of this because not much of that seems to hold great importance and yet, as Corley once quoted Hemingway to me, 'Every man's life ends the same way. It is only the details of how he lived and how he died that distinguish one man from another.'

After coming home I struggled on for another year with the agency, still working a desk but one whose importance diminished on a daily basis, and then, to use the current terminology, we had a 'conscious uncoupling' and I moved into the Foreign Service where I stayed for the duration of my career, slowly climbing rungs, my advancements marked by the rising quality of my suits and a greater understanding of how power administrates itself. I think I had a natural affinity for diplomacy that at the end of the day is always merely the advocacy of civilised relationships, predicated exclusively, of course, on self-interest. I learned how to smooth paths and how to convey insight, even sagacity, saying as little as possible when opinion wasn't required. In those early years I also kept the fact that I continued to read a private matter, because in the world I moved in there were those who saw contemporary fiction as a honey trap and in their narrow vision was probably the equivalent of sleeping with the enemy.

Coupled with organisation and efficiency, and I suppose my inherent 'steadiness', I was able to make my way until, in the fullness of time, I acquired a reputation for sound judgement. For prudence. Perhaps even for patriotism, although I like to think I wore it as lightly as the Stars and Stripes pin in my lapel. And if the younger staff occasionally whispered to newcomers that I was one of the last out of Saigon, I did nothing to diminish that little flush of admiration that in REMF world is offered to those who have seen service. One of the last out. It makes me smile to think of the number of times I have been assured by individuals – mostly in late-night bars or on long-haul flights when the lights are finally dimmed – that they were on that final rooftop chopper and I simply nod and wonder, if everyone's claim was true, how it would ever have been able to lift itself into the air. The only reality revealed by such stories is that some suffer from the desire to recast themselves as a hero, a desire that thankfully I have felt no need of in my life and hope to avoid now.

My career saw me move at intervals around capital cities, although sadly never Paris, and I had my longest posting in London that my friends tell me permanently anglicised me. I met Julia in London. She was a curator in one of the city's smaller museums and we encountered each other at a temporary exhibition the Embassy was sponsoring. I liked her right from the start and after a year's courtship we got married. My parents and sister flew in for the wedding – it was the first time my parents had ever been outside their own country and they seemed both disorientated and excited by the adventure. Julia proved a good partner in every way and took to the diplomatic life with a polished ease – sensitive, intelligent, and with a good supply of humour that shored me up at various times when it was needed, or when my inherent anxieties rose too close to the surface. She was someone who didn't like fuss and wasn't interested in getting involved in any of the petty disputes and rivalries that sometimes characterise the world of diplomatic wives who can give the impression they are longing to be in a rerun of *Peyton Place*. Our marriage was mostly happy but, despite Madame Binh's distant prophecy, produced no children. If I don't like to talk about her too much it's because she was someone who valued her privacy and there is also a reluctance to bring her into a story when it involves so many things in which she played no part. So out of respect and out of love I try to keep her in a separate place in my memory, untouched by what else needs to be told.

There is only one memory I want to share. In 1995 I was part of Clinton's entourage when we flew into Northern Ireland where we had played a pivotal part in the Peace Process and after tortuous negotiations produced an agreement that most of the main players could put their name to. Julia came too – she had family in the North and took the opportunity to introduce me to a bewildering number of aunts and uncles, distant cousins. On the night when the President switched on the Belfast Christmas tree lights, huge crowds turned out, buoyed up on the optimistic embrace of peace. The city was bedecked in lights, Van Morrison sang 'Days Like This' and Julia insisted we watch not from the windows of the City Hall but stand with the crowd. There was a sense of pride in what some labelled American 'soft power', although I don't think of it in this way. When the President made his later speech in Derry, he quoted the lines by Seamus Heaney about a once-in-a-lifetime moment when hope and history rhyme and just for a time we felt as if we had brought something good into existence. Now, of course, they have floundered into recurring stalemates, that precious momentum lost, and we are left to wonder if, rather than that rhyme of hope and history, we have what Heaney in one of his poems in *North* called 'exhaustions nominated peace'. But that night as I stood with Julia we experienced an intimacy with each other and with those around us that made us believe, however falsely, that the future could blossom into everything our hopes might conceive.

My uncoupling from the intelligence services was never allowed to develop into a full-blown divorce – once they have you, they don't easily let go – and at intervals I was asked for certain favours. Introductions, the opening of doors, occasionally the closing of doors and the clearing-up of mess, the unofficial use of the Embassy's facilities for purposes I didn't need or wish to know about – these were the most common requests. Once, during a very early placement like some le Carré Cold War spy, I had to take a train journey across Berlin and glad-hand a potential defector at a prearranged rendezvous, complete with code words and items of identification, but such amateur dramatics were thankfully rare. I think they always knew my heart wasn't in it.

After retirement from the Foreign Service I found my time and supposed expertise on distant lands, partly as a consequence of my two books, in regular demand. I advised a range of Congressional committees, helped produce endless numbers of reports and investigations, developed a close relationship with the Democrats. I acquired an apartment down in Washington that I continue to maintain and liked to think I had the ear of at least some of the Capitol's players. When I lost Julia I took on most of the invitations that were offered, thinking that keeping busy might prove the best way to ward off the paralysis of grief. But after a few years the unmitigated meaninglessness of pretending insight into an increasingly fragmenting and anarchic world left me weary and despondent and so I retreated to the coastal house that was to be our final resting place. Now, some days, the only person I engage with is Hannah, and if she knew how much that has started to mean to me she would ask for double what I pay her to act as my housekeeper.

I can't see the ocean from the house but somehow I always know it's there, and not just when storms worry the shoreline because it manages to salt along the blood-lines, nestles its restless murmur in the inner ear, so even when I walk the city's streets I think I can hear it assert itself over whatever traffic rushes by. Sometimes I stroll the beach, offer brief good mornings to the dog walkers and exchange polite nods with the joggers who have no surplus breath to respond in words.

In the last month I have walked it more often than usual, because it feels like a good place to think and perhaps hoping that the vastness that stretches so endlessly might serve to absorb the things that are troubling me, but as I stand and watch the waves break they seem only to press anxieties even deeper.

It was when walking the beach, about a month ago, that I first realised I was being watched. At the start I supposed it was the legacy of spending too much career time around spooks and laughed it off as a manifestation of my ingrained fears. But it wasn't past experience that warned me, so much as the sixth sense that we all possess and which has the ability to triumph over even the most skilled fieldcraft. So the man on the boardwalk in sweats and Nikes turned his attention to his newspaper slightly too studiously when I glanced towards him, and his companion loitering by the kiosk with the cup of coffee somehow failed to convince in his adopted pose of casual indifference to all around.

On one of those first mornings I went for a coffee in Gino's Seafront Diner that does a good line in bagels and lunchtime chowder. It's a pleasant spot where no one minds if you linger and the waitresses are enough of an age and disposition that an older man can smile at them without it making him feel creepy. I took a window seat and pretended to focus on my local paper, reading about the ongoing battle between environmentalists and a fracking company in pursuit of new planning approval, but at the same time watching out for those I suspected were following me. After a minute one of them entered and took a booth in a corner. I let my eyes rest on him just long enough to see him looking at me over the top of the menu before he looked away, and to register that his clothes were at just the slightest of variances to those of the locals. I finished my coffee and went outside but almost immediately went back through the doors to retrieve the paper I had deliberately left. He had already stood up and then, encountering me, headed to the restrooms, the waitress still standing at his table with her pen poised. I hadn't imagined it, nor did I imagine that a black SUV with out-of-state plates always seemed parked up somewhere along the route of my daily walk from then on.

That morning, as I walked back home and caught the reflection of the black SUV in a store window, I felt the anger that always comes with a sense of betrayal. It was as if my years of service had been expunged from the record, as if all the preceding decades counted for nothing, and I had to stop myself from turning round and knocking on the glass of the car and demanding an explanation.

It finally made sense when Corley – Corley Rodgers – suddenly made his presence known after an absence of almost forty years. After Saigon he had actually written his novel – I had winced at the universally unkind reviews it mustered – but he hadn't married Sylvia. Despite my assurances, she had indeed dumped him, but, displaying a greater sense of ambition than he had attributed to her, passed on the gym and geography teachers and hooked up with the principal himself. That turned out to be not such a major heartbreak, for not long after Corley admitted to himself that he was in fact gay and, as I learned later, found happiness of sorts in a couple of long-term relationships. He also admitted to himself that he wasn't a writer and took up a career in film-making. Our paths never crossed but when, subsequently, curiosity got the better of me I found him online. He made mostly low-budget documentaries and his name appeared at the smaller festivals or shortlisted for some minor prize he never actually won. To finance his film ventures he produced advertising videos and promos for various corporate interests, despite the subject matter of his own films often being radical in their motivation.

Eventually, after much calling in of favours, I heard from a source in journalism that the word was that Corley had gone underground and had established a relationship with a former security operative who was going to sing like a canary about various covert operations, about renditions and tortures, and that it was all going to be posted on the Web.

Although I can't be certain, I think he might have tried contacting me by phone – a couple of late-night calls that I didn't take because the number was withheld. A phone that I now assume is being tapped.

But he has eventually succeeded in coming back into my life – not in person, but with the package that arrived a few days ago in the post and now sits on my desk. In it is a DVD and a note that says, 'Mikey, thought you'd be interested in this. Stay with it to the end, your friend Corley.'

There isn't even a postal or email address included and, as I hold it in my hands, at first I imagine that I am being given something to admire, something that is to redress a real or imagined deficit that has accrued from the past, the way occasionally you encounter rather nondescript former acquaintances who want to let you know that, despite your supposed, never actually declared judgement of them, they have subsequently made good and offer the evidence to prove it. I haven't rushed into watching whatever is on it because what feels like an invitation to resurrect our shared past isn't entirely welcome and the uncertainty of where it might lead has seen me set it to one side, wanting to postpone this unexpected reunion.

But now, as the squall blusters about the house – feeling more like an expression of bravado rather than real threat – I finally take the DVD out of the envelope and sit down once more with Corley, Corley, Tell a Story Rodgers. And as the screen flickers into life, it seems to my surprise that what is unfolding in front of me isn't about our past or about whatever covert enterprises he is currently involved in. Isn't about the world we once knew. Not at the start.

A man sits at a kitchen table. His face is kept angled in shadow but what is visible is weather-beaten and lined with the imprint of a hard life. He might be in his early or mid-forties. He wears a denim shirt with little metal tips on the point of his collar that lend him the air of a cowboy, someone who has worked the land under the harsh scrutiny of the sun and wind. He is smoking, from time to time flicking the ash into a glass ashtray. His thick fingers have two rings. One appears to be a plain gold band, the other a topaz in a fancy filigreed setting. Behind him on the kitchen worktops are pots – one is cooking with skinny wisps of steam emerging. Beside the stove sit what looks like tortillas, a packet of cigarettes, a newspaper and a container of what might be cooking oil. The camera lingers over everything in a way that invites the viewer to invest meaning in the images. He is not a cowboy. He works as a mechanic, troubleshooting for haulage and construction companies. Always on call, day or night, skilled at getting broken-down machinery working again.

'How long have you been here?' the invisible interviewer asks.

'Five years,' he says, looking at his hand as if he needs to count the years on his fingers.

'And you have a good life here?'

'*Sí*, a good life. A house, a job,' he answers, without the enthusiasm that his words might be expected to generate. He lets his hand sweep round in a gesture that invites the camera to confirm what he has just said.

'But you miss your family?'

'*Claro.*'

'You have two children?'

'A son and a daughter.'

'What age are they?'

'Son twenty, daughter eighteen. My wife is dead.'

'You think of them often?'

'*Siempre, siempre.*'

'You're here illegally, aren't you?'

He nods imperceptibly then raises his right hand languidly off the table in a way that seems to suggest the question is unnecessary and that life has brought him where he is and in so doing it overrules whatever laws might exist. The gesture is not an apology so much as an expression of acceptance of the way things are.

'You crossed illegally?'

'Yes, I came with the *coyotajes*.'

'Was the journey difficult?'

He draws on the cigarette, then after considering the question nods slowly.

'A long walk through desert. Not easy. Not everyone made it on that crossing.'

'Tell me about it.'

He stubs out his cigarette with more force than is needed and it's unclear whether the frustration is at the question or caused by his memories. His face disappears, only his words are heard as we are shown images of a desolate landscape dressed in heavy brush, cacti, mesquite, and the camera follows little sanded pathways, stopping only to home in briefly on a scrap of clothing barbed on a bush or an empty water container.

'We had paid our money and went at night, crossing where we were told no guards would ever look. We followed the *coyotajes* for a long time. Very cold at night, hot during the day. You cannot carry all the water you need. Sometimes needles go through your boots. I see snakes. Sometimes we rest but not often enough for some of the group. The *coyotajes* smoke dope, which is a bad thing when a clear head is needed. Sometimes they laugh at something and I begin to think that they can't be trusted and that they are leading us nowhere and will disappear with our money into the darkness.'

In a clearing the camera pans around the debris of a crossing party – water canisters, empty cans, scraps of clothing, food wrappings, a half-covered sole of a shoe.

The camera lingers on them as if they are sacred objects. Everything in this film is slowed down. I hear a voice in my head saying, 'More matter, less art.'

'The second night we hear an engine some way far, but for sure an engine, and we have to scatter, hide in the brush. There are headlights and voices, but it passes on, and after an hour we start off again, but now our guides are gone and when we gather some are still missing. I never see them again. Never.'

His face is shown once more but still in shadow. He has lit another cigarette and the smoke trembles against the side of his face like a veil.

'And yet you have paid for your son and daughter to make such a crossing. Why?'

'There is no other way. They have no life except for this life that is here. And sometime, for sure, there will be an amnesty for all who crossed.'

'Why do you say that?'

'Because we work hard and that means we are needed. They will not send us back. *Nunca.*'

The camera shifts to the pot that's slowly simmering. And then we're somewhere else. An unnamed border town and the filming suggests it's been done surreptitiously as we walk past what look like impromptu stores selling the paraphernalia of crossing, as if offering to equip pilgrims for their coming journey, or the way commerce flourished to equip the gold rushes. So there are backpacks and water bottles, camouflage clothing and walking boots, blankets and hats to protect from the sun. An old woman with a wizened face and missing teeth smiles behind her stall and hopes for a purchase. Then there are shelters offering beds, cable television and hot water to those who have arrived and need a place to stay before they attempt the crossing. We go inside one – a communal room with bunk beds, a man sitting on one in a white vest who holds his hand in front of his face, a huddle of young men playing cards and listening to a radio.

A young man and a woman. His son and daughter. Again their faces are only partly revealed. And they speak softly and shyly in Spanish, as if making a confession to a priest, and the subtitles tell us that they are ready to make the crossing, ready to be part of the new and better life that their father has made.

'Are you frightened?'

The young woman looks at her brother before nodding, but he smiles and says, '*Solamente un poco.*'

They shall carry almost no personal possessions, only the provisions that they will need to survive. Their father has paid the price – seven thousand dollars for both of them and they know that if they are caught by a border patrol their father's hard-earned money will be lost. The young man says that where they live has become a ghost town, its life and future transported to a different world. Only the old and infirm are left. And the few – he struggles for the word, so he calls them *politicos* – who want the young to stay because their country needs them, because they can help build a better future for their people.

'But the cartels, the drug gangs, will not let it happen,' the young woman says, and then looks at her brother as if to see whether she has said something she shouldn't.

He stares at his hands and says nothing. We get a shot of their backpacks sitting ready in a corner. I grow impatient, think of fast-forwarding, more interested in understanding why Corley has sent me it, but I remember his admonition to watch to the end and so I let it run. So there is more about this brother and sister – their ambitions, their hopes for their future life, what they think America will be like. And then they are gone and we're listening to a cop sitting in a Volkswagen SUV pulled off the highway, his weight spread fully and loosely over the front seat. He's wearing mirrored shades and in appearance and manner he looks like he has evolved from Rod Steiger in *In the Heat of the Night*. And yes, they do their best with the limited resources they have but maybe those up north don't understand the nature of the problem. There are ripples of flesh circling his neck and as he grows animated they coalesce into a sac from which he seems to dredge the words. So despite the surveillance systems, motion sensors and drones, there's nothing can stop this influx except old-fashioned feet on the ground and an experienced cop's instincts. The border is a sieve, he claims, with so many holes that unless something changes their arrests are only a skim across the surface. He shifts his weight and holds on to the steering wheel to help him find a new balance, his eyes scanning each passing car as if it might be laden with illegals. Then he takes off his sunglasses and rubs his eyes as if they're weary of the constant surveillance. But there's one more thing he wants to say, which is that he's been part of body recovery and it's not something he wants to be doing until he retires. 'It ain't a pretty sight,' he says. 'Bloated bodies. Often scavengers have been at them before we find them. Not something you can shake easy out of your mind.' There is sky in the glasses he has put back on. 'Sometimes they're so remote you can't drive and you have to hike to where they've been found. Black body bags for the recently dead, white for skeleton remains. It's not a good experience to carry one of those bags – black or white, but especially black – to where you had to leave your vehicle.'

'How many bodies have you recovered?'

'Couldn't say exactly, but hundreds.'

'Hundreds?'

'For sure. Sometimes they get identified, sometimes they don't. And somebody south of the border is wondering when they're going to get in contact and somebody north is wondering the same. Maybe if some of them saw what we see, they would think twice about taking the risk.'

It is the type of stuff I feel I've seen before, even though the home-grown low tech somehow gives it a sharply personal edge. And then it becomes a drama, because we're back with the brother and sister packing what they need and telling the invisible interviewer that yes they know there are risks involved but maybe, the young man says, there are more risks in staying. They're young and fit. Others have made it, sometimes much older. Then we see hands fitting cameras, hidden cameras that will chart their attempt to cross, and I realise that we're going on the journey with them.

Is it drama or melodrama when the narrator's voice tells us that there are other dangers involved apart from being apprehended by the border patrols, and it speaks of people being forced to carry drugs across, of being abandoned as part of some shakedown and the possibility of encountering some of the recently formed militia groups who have sprung up ostensibly to volunteer assistance to the police, whether it's wanted or not? One of them, a rancher, appears on-screen standing in front of a cut fence as if it is the portal through which every immigrant has entered since the arrival of the Pilgrim Fathers. He's talking about a flood, of disease and crime, of potential terrorists, about an economy that can't support any more outstretched hands. And he's a patriot, and there's a growing number just like him, because if something doesn't change then it's going to be too late. As he's talking I can't help thinking of Tom Buchanan's advocacy of *The Rise of the Colored Empires* – strange how often moments in books still permeate my consciousness. But he's not a man to be sniggered about and you can tell that, unlike Buchanan, his hands have earned everything in the world he owns.

The clock is ticking. It's time to make the crossing. But first we see their father from behind, standing in an open doorway, one hand held high on its frame. So he's waiting, waiting with an open door, and then we're cut from that exterior shot of blue sky and in a shadowy world of pixelated faces so it's like some parody of *The Blair Witch Project*, and subtitles are used to capture the few words that are spoken and there is no voice-over so it feels as if we're separated from any familiar external world and are fully in only what we can discern from the grainy, jerky images. At times it resembles nothing so much as a shadow puppet play. And not for the first time I start to wonder about what Corley is doing and if he has any understanding of the potential danger that he has put this couple in. Later on a little research reveals the film generated its own in-house controversy when it was intimated by unnamed sources that the father, brother and sister were all actors, and I had a sudden memory of that night in Saigon when he told me he didn't know the difference any more in what was true and what was made-up.

But as I watch the couple clamber down from the back of a truck and crowd in with about twelve other individuals, they are real people to me and, as intended, I'm involved with their fates. The subtitled instructions are simple – stay together, don't make noise and do whatever you're told. Anyone who wants to go back should do so now but no one will bring you back if you go ahead. '¡Entiende, entiende!' whispers round the huddle and heads nod. The soundtrack to the march is the shuffle of feet through sand and heavy breathing as the pace increases. Sometimes a foot snaps something brittle or a thorn bush tears at a coat. Once there is what sounds like a dog barking in the distance. There is a shot of a momentarily frozen rabbit with startled neon eyes. The pictures fade out – real time is too long for an audience. When they return we see the group at silent rest in a brush-circled clearing. Some drink from various containers. And then they're on the move again in single file, leading to mostly shots of someone's back. A digital clock appears in the bottom of the screen to make us aware of how much time is passing without the necessity of seeing every step. We've never been told where they are, so perhaps it's the Sonoran Desert or one of a hundred other crossing places. And then many hours later there is the sudden flare of a spotlight and an amplified voice telling them to give themselves up and a rush of panic as the dark figures scatter in all directions. Feet stumbling in the loose sand in a burst of heavy breathing. Backpacks slapping against the shoulders of each of the runners. Brush being pushed aside. Clothes being plucked and snagged. The camera fades.

The camera stays faded into darkness until we get a reprised shot of the father standing at his open door. Looking out at unbroken space, cloudless sky. His hand drops slowly from the frame. The door is closed. Very poetic, Corley. Although perhaps a little too obvious with its symbolism. And I still haven't seen anything that is pertinent to me and start to wonder if it is just as I originally imagined, an exercise in catch-up on his part, a decades-late attempt to self-justify when in truth he doesn't need to prove anything. But just as the writing on the screen tells us that the brother and sister failed in their attempt at crossing but intend to try again, then fades, and suddenly I am startled by my own personal subtitled message instructing me to look closely at unused footage.

It's some kind of emergency station constructed by one of the ranchers who owns some of the land that is frequently used by those who cross. There are water barrels, tinned food, printed maps in different languages and lists of phone numbers, but most surprisingly of all there is what looks like some kind of totem pole. The camera traces its form in close-up. It is slender, about eight feet high, and appears to be a combination of carved wood and ceramic mosaic. The tile colours are blue and green with lines of mirrored glass and frequent inserts of shells and what might be slivers of bleached bone. There is a short crosspiece a foot from the top that is fringed with feathers. We are given no explanation as to what the pole is or its purpose. The light frazzles on the tiles and dances back against the camera. Is it some ancient religious artifice? But why is it here with the water and supplies? And it's not the only one because, as the camera pans across the landscape, more appear. Perhaps it's some burial ground. Then we're looking over the bars of a wooden gate at an adobe-style ranch building with white walls and a veranda. A woman, possibly Mexican, possibly partly Native American, with waist-length silver hair, is walking towards the camera waving her arms and telling whoever is filming to leave, that they are trespassing and have no right to be there. A man lurks on the veranda, a dog lapping round his legs, and then it comes towards the gate and begins to bark. The camera ignores it and focuses on the man. It brings his face into close-up and then freeze-frames. The subtitles ask me if I recognise anyone. At first I don't. All the changes, the ravages of unforgiving time, and then I shake my head, not because I don't but because I do, and as I sit staring at the frozen screen I slowly realise that the face belongs to Ignatius Donovan.

What does it mean to have this sudden and unexpected re-emergence from the past of two former men whose existence until this moment has been confined to my memory? My default mode is anxiety, of not feeling safe, and I feel that rising steadily. I like if at all possible to have my past under some kind of control in my head, but the appearance of these two revenants threatens that attempt at self-sustaining composure.

Corley's contact, however tentative, has placed me, if not exactly under suspicion of complicity – I like to think my unblemished CV would surely allay such a crude conclu-sion – but no doubt, with others, I am being watched in the hope that they will eventually catch him making further contact and before he does whatever it is that they fear so much. Part of me wants to simply walk up to the black SUV and tell them that I don't know where my former friend is in the world, but then I ask myself whether I would tell them if I did know and suddenly am not sure of the answer. And it's because everything in this life gets more compli-cated when the personal gets involved, no matter how much time and effort the system gives to depersonalising the contexts in which they wish you to operate. So even history itself is no longer laid out before you in accessible objective facts but becomes jumbled and coloured in your memory by the intensely personal shimmer of things that passed through your being, almost like light slowly filtering through the stained glass of seemingly random moments recalled. But without an overall design or pattern, so that it's impossible to make full sense of it. And while these fragments from the past are inconsequential in comparison to the broad sweep of events, and despite their supposedly lesser significance, they are what linger in the memory and continue to shape the view we have of ourselves and what happened to us.

So when I think now of Saigon all these years later, it is not a montage of all the political and military realities of that ill-fated episode in our national history that I dwell on, but rather a woman asking me to marry her daughter, black snow falling from a cloudless blue sky, my eyes briefly meeting those of a prisoner, the colourless silhouette of a butterfly on a canvas awning. Twelve spies went to spy in Canaan; ten were bad, two were good. But who can ever say inside the churning maelstrom of history and memory's distortions which we really were? And who can say if what took place all those years ago still shapes who we are today?

As for Corley, I think of him as a friend in only the most tenuous of ways, the long decades of separation enough to cast doubt on any belief that anything substantial still remains. But would I give him up? I would prefer, of course, that I never have to make the choice and so avoid arriving at a definitive conclusion, but if I can't escape that moment then perhaps, and even to my own surprise, I think that I wouldn't. If things happen and they are very bad things, then we have a right to know, even if ultimately we are prepared to accept them in the belief they are necessary for the greater good. If it stopped the planes flying into the towers. If it made our world safer. But I know, too, that nothing is ever that simple and mostly the idea of the greater good is merely a camouflage to do things we don't want anyone to know about. And there is another thought, however self-interested it might seem, and it's if things are allowed to happen in the far-flung dark corners of the world, then sooner or later they happen in the home place. And from all those distant days I remember Donovan's words that though the sheep fear the wolves it's the shepherd who kills them.

It isn't Corley, however, I find myself thinking about in the hours that follow, but rather Ignatius Donovan. Somehow, even though I struggle to acknowledge it, I know that despite the passage of years, and all the times I've tried to deny it, a part of my consciousness bears the imprint of Donovan, despite wanting nothing more than to erase it. And thinking about Ignatius Donovan gave me a kind of permission to think also of Tuyen. If the truth has to be told, I have often thought about her, even on occasions constructing an alternative life that begins with her sitting beside me on that flight out of Saigon. It is a story that my imagination has often woven, threading it through the most secret moments of my daily existence and always ending with a desire to know what happened to her. Was it just some poor man's tired Madame Butterfly fantasy, or because, as I have found out, loneliness is the powerful instigator of many forms of divergent thoughts and behaviours? Had Donovan helped her get away, helped her escape with the child she was carrying? The reality of his own family and Quyen's conviction that he had abandoned them argued against that possibility, yet he had gone to their home looking for them. And when in moments before sleep or on the slow hours of plane journeys I try to imagine the life we might have shared, it is always stifled by guilt then superseded by the love I found with a different woman. There have even been times when I have thought of making discreet enquiries, but both the magnitude of that task and a fear of disturbing the pattern into which my life had settled prevented me.

Hannah has sensed my preoccupation this morning and has already asked twice if I'm OK. I tell her I'm fine and then change the subject by asking about her boys. Tyrone is in college and I'm pleased to be able to help sponsor him. Charles is another story, however, and on at least one occasion I've had to speak on his behalf after he got himself into petty scrapes with the law. Sometimes when my mind slips into fantasy, as the mind is always able to do despite the encroachment of age, I think of asking Hannah if she'd consider being something more than a housekeeper. In my imagination of course she always says yes and so in these, my later years, I refind the comfort of companionship, of sharing a life with someone. Of having someone with whom you can experience tenderness and kindness. But it's a question I'm never going to ask because the reality is that it's my fantasy, not hers, and it frightens me to think of losing her. So I content myself with snatches of conversation, the noise of her busying herself in the kitchen and knowing that, as with every other day, it will end with the sound of her car setting off down the drive.

She's knocked on my study door, even though it's open, and is standing with a cup of coffee. It's a room she never comes into, for some reason, so I go to the door and take the cup from her, try not to look too long into her eyes.

'Thanks, Hannah,' I say, as I do regularly throughout every one of her visits, and then I tell her that I'm going to take a trip, that I'll be away for three or four days. Perhaps five.

'Washington again?' she asks, out of what I know is politeness rather than curiosity, and I say yes even though it's not where I'm going. And as I finally allow myself to look at her, I understand that time imposes no limitation on need, that it never withers on the vine, and I don't know whether this is a source of embarrassment or a vestige of life itself for which I should be grateful.

So what is it that sees me on a plane and flying towards my past? The need to know? The need to tie up loose ends? Perhaps both these things, but always something more. Something that's hard to define. Part of it is being in a Saigon room with a mother asking me to marry her daughter, to be a father to her child, and despite the moral code that I've always thought I tried to live by, my inability to know what was right or whether I was brave enough to meet its demands head-on. And always somewhere in the back of my mind that same unanswered speculation about the course my life might have taken and whether it would have been for better or worse. There is, too, something else that gradually and reluctantly makes itself known — a need to see Donovan again, to stand before him no longer the naive young man subservient to his every order, to stand before him and let him see who I became, who I am, even though there is something shameful about wanting the approval of someone you despised.

So where exactly am I heading? No names, no pack drill. Old habits. On a need-to-know basis, I guess, and it takes a week or so to establish my destination, and after a little bit of my own hastily recalled and pretty rusty fieldcraft, a flight west and a few nights in motels that offer not much more than a clean bed and cold drinks out of vending machines. It's not possible to journey in America without coming to believe that we are a nation in flux, a people hurrying hither and thither, driven by the complexities of our existence and in pursuit of whatever place might let us think of it as home – a vision that is itself constantly changing and not always destined to be fulfilled. So in the airport departure lounge I meet a woman taking her ailing husband on one final trip to Vegas, as if hoping a change in fortune might be found in the holy spin of a ball or the grace-filled turn of a card; in a service station over a coffee I watch a college basketball team on their way to some tournament stretch their legs in the parking lot and shoot imaginary hoops, their lithe jumps like some slow-mo ballet; a modern-day Joad family piling back into their beat-up Winnebago and about to set out to wherever they think a better life awaits; and of course those legions of trucks on every road I travel, seemingly all of them decked in various flags and slogans, their good-luck charms and talismans. In the same service station I pause for a few seconds to look at the collage of faces on MISSING posters, some of them children, all of their eyes looking out towards some irrevocably altered future, and then as I turn away a woman hands me a flyer advertising a gospel campaign and telling me that the wages of sin are death. I say thank you and keep walking, slip it into my pocket, and as I continue my journey I feel as if I too am part of this relentless flux, cut loose from the established and secure moorings of my own life, but heading towards something that may be nothing more than a mirage.

Eventually, steeped in weariness and coming closer to the end of my journey, I find myself bumping over dirt roads in a hired SUV, the sun slicing through scrub and semi-desert so that its frazzling brightness hurts the eyes. I am voyaging through a part of the continent unfamiliar to me and which seems intensely distant from the world I know. I experience a stark sense of dislocation and wonder if I have set out on the most futile and misguided of impulses, marked by misdirections, miscalculations, an almost accident with a riderless, careering horse, and suspicion in the eyes of anyone I ask for help in pointing the way. The last of these a Marlboro Man, his face like dried-out hide with creases so deep that dust could layer itself on the ledges of his skin, who shakes his head in response and then spits with a vehemence designed to suggest that no one of any worth would be going to the destination I had enquired about. But however long and arduous the journey, it is nothing compared to the rapid migration through time I have been making as memory threatens to overpower the present.

Finally, despite the confused satnav and a printed map seemingly designed to hide rather than reveal, I arrive at the entrance to a ranch that I see with a jolt is named Canaan, the letters formed in a ceramic mosaic built into stone pillars, the tiles dust-smeared and chipped. And as I drive through and head down a long dirt track without a dwelling in sight, it seems to me not that I am entering a

Promised Land but some remote Charles Manson hideout from where I might never return. But as I venture further I know I have finally come to the right place because, turning a bend, I pass the same type of poles seen in the video. Again, about eight feet high, constructed from wood and decorated with ceramic tiles, and garlanded with wreaths of feathers, bones and shells. There are words written in different places but too small to be read from my distance.

The house itself is made from stone and wood, the lineaments of some old adobe still distinguishable at its core, with more modern appendages added on in a haphazard way. To both sides are outbuildings, including something that almost resembles a barn, and beside it a corral where four horses fidget and flick their heads at flies. A veranda shadows the house frontage, so when I pull up I don't see him at first and when I get out into the flaring heat of the sun it is only his disembodied voice I hear.

'You're a long time coming, Mikey. Almost thought you weren't going to make it. Welcome to Canaan.'

He steps into the parabola of light and I look at him in the flesh for the first time in over forty years and for a second time struggle to recognise him. Dressed in jeans and a plaid shirt, the strength of body that once distinguished him has deserted, leaving a gaunt figure, his face sun-spotted and grizzled. He stands with hunched spindle shoulders, his thin neck a stretch of tightened skin. He wears a red bandana and his hair has long gone, only the faintest smear on his temples hinting at its former colour. This old man no longer bears any resemblance to the Ignatius Donovan I once knew so much as a braidless tribute act to Willie Nelson, marooned in a desert waste land. But when he called me Mikey the cadence was exactly the one with which I was familiar and suddenly time finally collapses in on itself, the decades rushing from my grasp like a deck of cards in free fall. His voice speaking my name ricochets in my memory, bouncing off things I had heard him say, the conversations in his car and elsewhere, and so, despite his appearance, in the single use of that word I find myself slipping back through all the intervening years into the relationship we once had, regardless of my determination to establish something utterly different.

'Come aboard, Mikey,' he says. 'Step inside out of the heat. Meet Melissa.'

He doesn't offer his hand, and I don't extend mine, but he opens the door that is decorated with beads, a small bleached animal skull and tin star and moon shapes that look like they've been hammered out of empty Coke cans. Inside is shadowy but the restricted ingress of light shivers dust motes so it almost feels as if a fine rain is sifting down. A woman with long silver hair – the woman in the video – stands in front of an open fireplace where half-burnt blackened logs litter the darkened space. She comes forward and offers me her hand whose every finger seems to wear a silver ring and as she stretches it towards me I hear the soft clink of her bracelets.

'Welcome,' she says. 'You must be thirsty. A cold drink? Tea, beer … ?'

'Give Mikey a beer,' Donovan says. 'He was always a hard-drinking man.'

'You've mistaken me for someone else,' I say, 'but I'll take a beer.'

He signals me to sit down and I take a place on a blanket-covered settee that has a dog sleeping soundly at the other end who goes by the name of Charlie. We are in a room that, like the building itself, is a mixture of many different and seemingly disconnected objects and styles sharing only a relentless shadowy shabbiness. On the walls at intervals are abstract paintings but with a range of other materials added to them – stones, dried seed heads, animal bones, emblazoned hand prints. In other places there are crudely made masks with missing eyes. One wall is covered with old yellowing maps but I can't decipher where they depict. I feel disorientated again, not in possession of the calm self-confidence that I assumed would prevail, but when Melissa returns with the beers I affect a relaxed composure and make some small talk about my problems finding the ranch.

'Out of sight, out of mind,' Melissa says.

'Don't you believe it,' Donovan says. 'We're all being watched now. Every second of the day. Isn't that right, Mikey?' But before I can reply he continues, 'Our phones, computers, everything we say, all being fed into rooms to be logged and analysed. You know something, Mikey? There are nights, when the world is sleeping, I can hear the voices singing in the wires, carried in the hum of electricity across the empty stretches of the darkness.'

'And can you hear what the voices are saying?' I ask, trying not to smile.

'There's no way of hearing the words because it's so many voices. It's the world's babel, Mikey. A confusion of tongues. But they're always there, spinning and coursing through the darkness.'

'Maybe the voices come from inside your head?' Melissa offers.

'Sure they do – everyone's got voices in their head,' he says. 'But these aren't my voices, the ones I recognise, but a flow out of the universe, the world speaking in tongues.'

He sips his beer and stares into space as if contemplating something more important than me, and in those few moments I'm compelled towards a startled reassessment. I have come – foolishly of course – with an impression of the Donovan I knew in Saigon, seemingly fixed permanently in my memory, and yet already I am looking at someone a world away from those ingrained images. But it isn't just about the passing of time, even though if he resembles anything at all it's some New Age hippie, or even one of the original Haight-Ashbury crew trapped in aspic, washed up by the tide of history and beached in this nowhere place that seems to exist without recognisable coordinates or any connection to the person I once knew.

'I'll fix us some food,' Melissa says before disappearing again.

'How long have you been together?' I ask.

'In this world and worlds to come,' he answers, and the gnomic riddles with which he peppers his conversation seem as explanatory to him as they are incomprehensible to me. 'Her people are the original inhabitants of this land and she holds a deep affinity for it, can trace its ley lines with her spirit. Knew too where we would find water. You know, Mikey, what the Bible says about such a woman?'

I shake my head because my once acute Bible knowledge has faded a little with disuse and my memory feels hazy, in part caused by the confusions unfolding all around me.

'"Who can find a virtuous woman? For her price is far above rubies. The heart of her husband doth safely trust in her, so that he shall have no need of spoil. She will do him good and not evil all the days of her life. She seeketh wool, and flax, and worketh willingly with her hands. She considereth a field, and buyeth it: with the fruit of her hands she planteth a vineyard. She stretcheth out her hand to the poor; yea, she reacheth forth her hands to the needy."'

His voice seems drawn from somewhere deep inside himself and when he speaks it takes on an incantatory feel that is accentuated by a slight rocking back and forward. For those few seconds he seems far away, oblivious to my presence, and then, returning, he looks at me, as if seeing me for the first time, before asking, 'And have you been blessed with a wife?'

'My wife has died but yes I was blessed,' I tell him.

'That blessing will never leave you, Mikey. It will stay with you all the days of your life.'

And I remember Madame Binh telling my fortune and it feels once more as if I am sitting with someone convinced of their mystical powers of insight when everything else I know about them suggests that they live exclusively inside whatever distorted reality they have constructed. And what silently shakes me is that, while to all appearances Donovan might have shed his former self, he still feels able to assume the role of my mentor, the imparter of the knowledge he assumes I lack. A relationship I want to break free from once and for all.

'How did you end up living here?' I ask.

'A life twists and turns,' he says, 'until, if you let it, and if you hold yourself in readiness, it leads you to where you need to be.'

'So how long have you been here?'

'Heading towards twenty years.'

'And you left the Service?'

'The Service left me, Mikey,' he says, looking at the darkened fireplace. 'I'm going to light it later. It can get cold at night. Seeps into your bones. I was involved with Eagle Claw when we tried to bring the hostages out of Iran. As you can imagine, that clusterfuck didn't promote anyone's career. Somebody had to take the rap. I was just one of many fall guys. They did me a favour, Mikey. Opened my eyes to things that had been hidden to me.'

'What kind of things?'

'That I was serving the wrong master.' And then, turning his eyes directly to me, he adds, 'Like we both were.'

Without speaking, I hear myself repeating different things in response and none of them sound exactly what I want to say, whether it's some naively patriotic assertion about serving my country or even an attempt at a joke. It's not an easy thing to negate your own life, to sneer away all the long years of service, and I'm not going to do it, but as I sit there everything seems to summon those days in Saigon that feel now as if they are rushing towards me. And in the word 'we' our two lives have been suddenly conjoined once more when I believed that everything that had happened since that shared time had sundered them forever. So at first I say nothing and the only sound is Melissa moving in the kitchen, the rattle of pots and the low hum of her voice in some barely registered melody.

'Afterwards the Ayatollah said the angels of Allah had kept them safe. And, Mikey, maybe they did. Who can say? You believe in angels, Mikey?'

'Not angels with wings. But I've met good people.'

'And then maybe they were angels. Because in this world sometimes we entertain angels unaware. It's something we should never forget.'

I offer nothing in response and instead try to focus on some of the questions I want to ask, but it is as if he senses what I'm thinking.

'There's things you want to ask, want to say, but let's save it for later. After we've eaten. When you've had time to rest. And you must stay here tonight.'

I tell him that I intended driving back in a few hours but he stiffens on the chair and straightens.

'It's not safe out there, Mikey. You must stay here until the morning. Melissa's already put your bag in the room at the end of the hall.'

'Why's it not safe?' I ask.

'There's people out there who wish us harm. White supremacists, young bucks dressed up in camouflage gear, a sprinkling of ex-vets, and some just because they take pleasure in hunting and don't care who gets caught in their cross hairs. Vigilantes, renegades – all the devil's servants. It's not safe because men love darkness rather than light. And there are others too – the voices on the wires, whispering their secrets to each other; the listeners, Mikey. And they probably already know you're here just like they know everything.'

Many things have changed with Donovan but I feel vaguely pleased that his paranoia remains untouched by whatever it is has altered the rest of him. He holds the bottle of beer in front of his face, looking at the world through its clouded glass. In the subsequent silence he rocks again, nodding slightly as if in a confirmation of something important to himself.

After a few minutes the silence becomes oppressive.

'You seem to have changed a lot,' I venture, suddenly unsure of what I should call him, and he looks at me as if aware of my presence for the first time.

'The whole world is changing, Mikey – everything in the universe is changing and so we need to change if we're to go on living. But how do you think I've changed?'

I don't know what to say. It isn't even possible to make some bland reference to the physical changes I've seen without stumbling into insensitivity and potential mutual embarrassment. But I'm a diplomat by instinct as well as career so I simply say, 'In your thinking about things.'

'My thinking about things? Well here's the thing, Mikey – I once was someone who didn't think. Everything that was in my head and came out of my mouth had been put there by Uncle Sam, by the secret, mind-destroying motherfuckers who don't want anyone ever to think for themselves. Because the first time a man starts to think for himself his only desire will be to drive a stake through their black hearts.'

The conversation peters out again and the intervals of silence stretch longer. I try to fill the gaps with small talk but he barely responds and sometimes when he looks at me it is as if he's struggling to recognise me. It's a relief when Melissa eventually summons us. We eat the simple meal she has prepared, preceded by his rambling grace expressing the hope the world will heal itself. Then the beers turn into whiskies and the three of us go outside with our glasses and sit on the veranda. After a few seconds Melissa goes inside and when she returns it's with a rifle that she leans against Donovan's chair.

'Coyotes come out at night,' he says, moving his hand along the barrel. 'Coyotes howling at the moon. Always best to be prepared, Mikey.'

We sit and stare out as night approaches and lends the landscape the appearance of a solitary moonscape with an opalescent striated light, and I feel as if I have travelled to the very boundary of my known world and even perhaps to the edge of my known self. Then for some reason I remember Donovan once telling me what his father had said about the moon landing, and how it was a hell of a long way to go to know what loneliness feels like, and, even as I sit there with two others, I experience my own loneliness shifting towards me from the shadowed wilderness that stretches far beyond what my eyes can see. It is silent, too, apart from the white noise of the cicadas and the occasional shuffling and whinnying of the horses. Melissa says very little except to ask me some questions about my family and where I was born. Her long hair looks silvered deeper by the moon. I couldn't say what age she is, although probably a little younger than Donovan, and her face has a calmness that contrasts with his frequent animation. After a while she goes inside again but later I glimpse her moving through the shadows towards the barn.

The wild scatter of night stars seems to have shocked the universe into a sense of wonder and gradually it feels like the time has come to ask some of the questions that have seen me make this journey across the country, but I know already I have drunk more than I am accustomed to and this simple fact, combined with a growing confusion, blurs some of the pre-prepared sightlines along which I have envisaged this meeting. So already I feel less certain about its outcome, despite the number of times I have played it out in my head.

'You said I was a long time coming? It sounded like you were expecting me. Expecting me after all these years.'

'It doesn't matter how long it took – I always knew you were coming, Mikey, and what is time anyway but the twinkling of an eye. I knew you would come to the wilderness because the wilderness is where everything gets tested and the future gets faced. And because you always need to know you've done the right thing. Always, Mikey. You never had a get-out-of-jail card like the rest of us – sometimes I wondered what you thought would happen to you if you hadn't done the right thing. As you got older – and we've both got old – I guess the need to know just gets greater.'

He lifts the rifle and sets it on his lap, then runs his hand repeatedly along its barrel as if polishing it.

'You want to remember and I'm trying to forget. Isn't that the shit-kicking truth?'

'What are you trying to forget?' I ask, knowing I have reached the point when I want to push him, perhaps even cruelly, to – what's the word? – a confession, a correction, a setting of things back in balance. I try not to make unnecessary moral judgements – it was an unwelcome impediment to the type of work I once did – but I am close to making one in this moment because I want to hear the words in his mouth. And I know it isn't about redeeming the sins of our history, the things that were done, the bombs we dropped, the people we left standing on stairwells waiting for choppers that never came. For a young woman carrying his child. For all the names on the Wall. No, and despite the embarrassment I feel now I understand it is for something deeply personal, perhaps even hopelessly selfish, in the face of that greater history. It is for an abrogation of the insistencies that once governed our relationship. For, if not a validation of the young man I once was, but whoever it is I am now, and it is as if I finally need some acknowledgement that after all I had stood up straight and true in my own way and on my own terms, and in so doing had held fast to a greater truth than he ever had. That the meek had inherited the earth rather than the warmongers. And instead of speaking his words, as I did in that prison cell, my life has spoken in a voice of my own.

But there is no answer from Donovan because, as we sit staring into the wilderness, there is the sound of an engine and a sudden beam of headlights lasering the darkness before both vanish as quickly as they have come. Donovan jumps up and shoulders the rifle.

'Sons of bitches crawling out from underneath their stones. They want me out of here. Won't stop until they see me dead or gone. Just like Satan came to the wilderness. And I've heard there's a price on my head but that's a bounty no one's going to cash in except me.'

At first I file this blank cheque in the Bank of Donovan's Paranoia but then remember the vehemence of Marlboro Man and my initial certainty is slowly tainted by doubt.

The lights have died. Donovan moves his rifle from side to side as if covering invisible watchers under the stars that press their brightness against the black pleats of the night sky.

'They come sniffing round at night, looking for cross-overs, smashing help stations, spilling water. Spilling water in a desert, Mikey. That's who the sons of Satan are. Can you hear the voices?'

But I hear nothing and am not sure if the voices are in his head or the babel he imagines coursing along the wires criss-crossing the continent. I recognise, however, the intensity of his voice, hear it chime with the echoes stored in my memory, and know that there is still a flame burning at his core, and it makes me apprehensive because, like facing some forest fire, you can never be sure in what direction the wind might blow it. And the rifle makes me nervous. In a different context I would take it from him, resting my arm on his old-man's shoulder while telling him that everything will be all right. But I know that isn't possible and as he talks I think of the long arid hours I spent at my father's hospital bed when Alzheimer's rendered him disconnected and disorientated from his former resolute self, as he spoke in staccato random sentences, trying to recalibrate fragmented moments of consciousness, his words trapped in an endless loop. And it isn't because Donovan's words bear any resemblance to my father's but rather that they force me into the same role of passive listener, seemingly acquiescent to what can't be fully grasped or incorporated into any form of recognisable reality.

'Can you hear the voices, Mikey? Can you hear them?'

And whether to appease his insistence, just as I often did at my father's bedside, or because I think I actually can, I say I do. He goes back into the house and switches off all the lights then summons the dog, a shaggy indeterminate breed, and with a sudden gesture of his arm sends it scampering into the night.

'Step down. Keep in the shadows,' he tells me, and I follow him.

Melissa appears and I see she too is holding a rifle. They stand there shivering, thin and silvered as if negatives of themselves, and just as I am wondering how best to extricate myself from this increasingly alarming situation and write off my journey as a self-indulgent exercise in futility, I see a fire-tailed shooting star and then another. Except of course they aren't stars and, as they tremble and flare through the darkness, I know that they are

Molotov cocktails. They crash in a splurge and roar of flame but both fall far short of the house and in response Donovan and Melissa fire a volley of shots into the air. There is the sound of an engine starting and a momentary glimpse once more of headlights, this time veering into the distance.

'You OK, Mikey?' he asks, turning towards me.

'I'm OK,' I say, although I am pretty shaken. 'But don't forget I'm a REMF, a desk jockey. This isn't my kind of stuff.'

Donovan gestures us back into the house but keeps the light low, so we sit in semi-darkness and from time to time he goes to the side of the window and peers out. I need him to explain, but before I can ask any of the questions spinning round my head he jumps up.

'Charlie, where's Charlie?'

He hurries towards the door but Melissa springs from her seat and bars his way.

'No, Iggy. No! You can't go out there in the dark. He'll be all right. He's a smart dog – he'll find his way back.'

For a second it looks as if he is going to ignore her but she presses her hand against him and he stands as if stalled. Then she pulls him closer until he rests his head on her shoulder so that they are motionless. I should respect the privacy of the moment, but don't, because it is the first time I have ever seen him appear so vulnerable, even fragile, and as he stands leaning into her it looks as if she is sustaining him both physically and emotionally.

'I'll light the fire,' he says as he slowly pulls back from her embrace, 'sit with Mikey a while. He's come a long way so we have things to talk about. You go to bed. They won't come back tonight.'

She asks him if he's sure, and when satisfied he's all right she kisses him on the top of his head the way a mother might do with her child, then says goodnight and heads down a shadowed corridor, her soft steps accompanied by the light tinkle of her bracelets.

'A good woman,' he says.

'Above rubies,' I tell him.

'That's right. Above rubies.'

He bends down to light the fire but I can see how much the physical effort renders his movements slow and hesitant.

'Here, let me do that,' I say, and start to lift wood from the pile at the side of the hearth.

'Sure, Mikey. I forgot you were a Boy Scout.'

Using old newspapers and thinner sticks as tinder, I get it going, relieved to avoid a show of ineptitude and to see the straggly flames strengthen and flourish so I'm able to add larger bits of wood.

'It's how I aim to go,' Donovan says, staring at the fire.

'How you aim to go?'

'I'm not being buried – no one's putting me under the earth. I'm never leaving here in a box, Mikey. Melissa knows what to do – we've talked it through. There's a little hollow not far from here surrounded by rocks, almost a ring, and I've already got a pyre started. Add to it all the time. At night under the stars. That's how I'm going.'

At first I think it's some expression of bravado but the quietness of his voice belies that and I stumble into some clumsy expression suggesting that that day is some way off.

'Look at me, Mikey. I'm dying. Can't you see? A strong wind blows right through me. Cancer. And there's no get-out-of-jail card any more. No dodging this bullet.'

I express my shocked sympathy as best I can and in the moments of silence that follow I think of the afternoon when I watched him swim in the pool at Le Cercle Sportif and remember the flame of his hair disappearing and reappearing beneath the surface, the way the furious energy of his arms seemed to beat the water into submission. But callous as it might sound, does it change anything or just lend urgency to why I have come?

'What are you doing here, Iggy? You're clearly in danger.'

It is the first time I have ever used his Christian name and it sounds strange on my lips. The fire slithers shadows into the dark corners of the room while the sun-bleached wood hisses. At first he doesn't answer and I wonder if he has heard my question. He stares at the fire almost as if that is where he is searching the answer and then he looks at me and suddenly I think of the wind blowing through him, the spores it carries like seed heads, slowly drifting then settling beyond the reach of help or cure.

'The whole world's crossing over, Mikey. The whole world. You know that already. The sea's parting for them but sometimes it closes over them again. All of them trying to reach Canaan. And there's nothing anyone can do to stop it and we shouldn't try because the world is tilting and maybe it's a way of setting itself right. Of finding its balance once more. Of paying what's owed. You understand?'

I nod without fully grasping what is being said.

'All over this world people trying to reach Canaan. In boats, hidden in the backs of lorries, on foot across deserts like these. Crossing over. You want to know what I'm doing here. All the world's borders are broken and I'm helping them, Mikey, helping them cross over. Reaching out our hands to the needy. Some of them come this way across the desert – not all of them make it and there are times when it's their lost souls singing on the wires that I hear. Sad songs trapped forever on the wires from souls lost in limbo where no hands can pull them free. If they do reach here we help them on their journey, give them supplies and shelter.'

A sudden collapse of wood in the fire sends sparks scuttling up into the darkness. We sit and stare at it, made shadows of both our former selves by time – Donovan through his physical degeneration and metaphysical reinvention of himself, I also at the hands of time and something else to which I'm not able to give a name, but which feels like the slow seep of uncertainty into what I had previously thought of as conviction.

'Then we send them north. Just like the old days of the railroad, there's a chain of helping hands, passing them on from place to place until they find where they want to be and are able to finally disappear into new lives. And I'm crossing over soon too, Mikey, so there's things need to be done, things to be taken care off.'

I wonder where he envisages his new existence, if any, when it comes to that night under the stars. But I have no desire or need to know because I have already stumbled too far into his world once again and, yes, because many of the important moments of my life have been reflected by books, I have indeed already thought of Kurtz. But there are no heads on poles in Canaan, only help stations, water to drink and the promise of shelter. So this is no heart of darkness, no Charles Manson Spahn Ranch, and at that moment I start to conceive of it in the most obvious terms – a final repentance, an attempted atonement for past sins that could no longer be obliviated by a quick confession and an easy penance. And who can say he was crazy because perhaps all our lives should have a final atonement – an atonement for the things we regret, for all the times we fell short of our best selves. For having lived timidly too often and at the direction of others. And, yes, when we didn't do the right thing, even though we go on trying to make excuses for those failures. Each of us could make our own lists and sometimes I tell myself that writing this story is part of my personal act of contrition and if nothing else that alone makes it worthwhile.

So to speak of Saigon suddenly feels unseemly, like a dog looking at its own sick. Will compelling a dying man on that journey through the years amount to anything other than a futile confrontation with what had long vanished into history and could not be changed? Nor do I know whether the things that happened in those far-off days might be ameliorated by words uttered in the present, or if it is possible that the memory could be salved, however selfishly or too conveniently. I no longer feel able to make the judgements that I clutched securely when setting out and, as we sit in the fire's light, the sweep of history seems to unravel into nothing more than the never-ending days in which we lived. Days filled with both piety and shame but which can never be fully disowned no matter how much we try.

I go to say something to him but see his head slump on his chest and for a second I think he has gone, until I hear his shallow breathing and know that he is sleeping. I take the blanket off the couch and cover him with it, then make the fire safe. I find the room where I am to sleep and lie down on the single bed. I will start back home in the morning, enter once more the round of my life, try to find something to staunch the loneliness of the house in which I live and try also to keep moving forward, because I know not to do so will eventually risk my succumbing to whatever it is that corrodes the soul. And on the edge of a desert I know I want to face the sea again, absorb its restless unceasing motion, let the salt-laden breezes fill my lungs and stir me into the possibility of life's newness even in what I like to think of as early old age. But as I slowly drift into sleep it isn't the ocean I see but those two quivering arcs of fire and, despite my resolve to keep moving forward, in my dreams I walk once more through the open door of La Porte Bleue, hear my calling voice echoing in its silent emptiness. And then I dream of snow, dream of snow on the edge of a desert. But what is falling, suffocating the world, isn't white but rather black; and it doesn't drift dreamily down from some drowsy sky: instead it churns its darkening flakes from the multiplicity of incinerators that burnt on Saigon roofs and in back courtyards and whose fall always marks the end of empire.

In the morning Melissa is in the kitchen and there is the smell of coffee. When she asks me if I have slept well I say I have.

'Mikey, Iggy's going to want to go looking for our dog. There's no sign of him. Will you go with him? Watch his back.'

'Sure,' I say. 'Maybe it's just chasing jack rabbits.'

'I hope so.'

Donovan appears and we eat breakfast at the kitchen table. He seems more gaunt in the harsh light of morning, his cheeks sunken and the shamrock on his skinny arm withered and leached of colour. He hasn't shaved and the grey stubble coating his face looks like a layer of dust. He is quiet, seemingly preoccupied, but from time to time I am aware of him glancing at me, perhaps to register the changes that time has also wrought in me, perhaps because he is wondering what I am thinking about the things he said last night. Then when we finish Donovan fetches his rifle and hands me the other one.

'If it helps, think of it as just for show,' he says and I remember that last car ride with him through the collapsing chaos of Saigon, when I sat in the passenger's seat riding shotgun as we sped on our final journey together through a city whose walls were tumbling and everything that our intervention had sought to build was turning to dust before our eyes.

Melissa tells us to be careful and when Donovan opens the door I blink in the sudden flare of light and heat. A cloudless sky stretches taut and boundless and as I step out on to the porch everything conspires to make us seem small, stick men, whose few brief steps of a life will leave no print on the fierce supremacy of the landscape. My hired car is coated in a fine veneer of dust, as if it was abandoned a long time ago, and as I walk a few steps behind Donovan my attempts to scan the terrain are made difficult by the need to constantly shield my eyes from the reflected brightness that radiates from everything flung before us: rocks scattered like moon debris, a slew of larger boulders, and straggly vegetation that despite its thorns is briefly softer to look at. Donovan doesn't speak at first but stops from time to time to survey his wilderness kingdom. His shirt hangs loosely on him, as if unable to find the body inside it, and sweat glistens on the bald orb of his head.

'They must have thrown from over there,' he says, pointing with his rifle to a boulder field with exclamation marks of tall thin cacti. 'And be careful, Mikey, you don't stand on a snake. It's a long way to a hospital.'

As we walk I finally admit to myself that coming to Canaan has been a mistake, a foolishness that could never provide me with whatever it was I was looking for. With each step I resolve to take my leave as soon as we have finished the search and even the basic comforts of shabby roadside motels seem increasingly attractive compared to this trek through an inhospitable wilderness. I already know that I would never have made an original pioneer and from childhood I wanted only to escape the tyranny of vast spaces, sought to find some future intersection of love and a life of quiet happiness, books rather than a map acting as my compass. I try to make a silent joke with myself about serpents in the garden and the resulting knowledge of good and evil but it deconstructs itself into dust with every stumbling step through the twists of brush.

The man walking slowly ahead of me is dying and I know if I don't tell the truth about this fact then everything else risks fragmenting into something that makes all my efforts worthless. I'm not glad but at the same time it makes it possible for me to privately believe that when he dies I might finally be able to shake myself free from this part of my former life forever. Everything that occurred in that strange and disturbing period, even whatever happened to Tuyen and her unborn child, might disappear into the night sky, borne away by the smoke and flames. To be able at last to disavow Madame Binh's prediction that I would never leave. This is what I tell myself and I think of Hannah, who has started to preside over my heart as well as my house, and I wonder if there is a way I might find to express something that touches on my feelings without the risk of losing her in a moment of mutual embarrassment that can never be rescinded. But there is another thought, too, that maybe the mature judgement on which I have prided myself for so long has, without my fully realising it, started to slide and be governed by the unreliability and unpredictability of impulse. And who could say any more which was right?

Behind a tumble of boulders we find the body of the dog, fly-crusted and with its throat cut. Find it there with tyre tracks, cigarette butts and a disposable lighter. Donovan kneels beside it, his hand on its flank, and half-whispers, 'Sons of bitches,' again and again until it becomes part of his breathing as the thin stems of his shoulder blades press against his shirt.

'I'll go get a shovel,' I tell him but he stops me, saying that neither of us has what it takes to dig a grave in this sun-baked earth.

'Go to the house and get a blanket,' he orders, 'and tell Melissa he's been shot. That it was clean and quick. Make sure she stays inside.'

When I return with the blanket he uses it to completely wrap the body, then hands me his rifle and I follow him as he carries the dog about a hundred yards to the south of the house, his breathing heavier with every slowing step. I know where we have come right away – the circle of rocks, the pile of wood. This is the place where his body will depart the world and I watch him remove some of the wood from the pyre then nestle the dog in it. He tells me to wait and so I stand with the two rifles and try in vain to find somewhere that offers shade.

'Shoot the first son of a bitch that moves' was the instruction the last time he placed a gun in my hand, but as I look about me there is no sign of human life until my eyes catch one of the decorated poles as light pools and frazzles in its mosaic squares of blue glass and its feathered arms stir a little, although I feel no trace of a breeze. What are they supposed to be? What half-crazy impulse has seen it and all the others erected in this remote landscape? Then Donovan returns with a can of gasoline and splashes it over the wood. Melissa comes too and the three of us stand silently in front of the pyre until Donovan lights it and we have to step back from the sudden splurge of heat. They stand with their arms round each other's shoulders and I imagine it is not possible for any of us to be there in that place and that moment without anticipating what is coming down the line. I can't say how long he has been given but I sense it will be relatively short and that he himself has no will to drag it out.

When it is done we head back towards the house and they walk hand in hand while I carry the two rifles. The smell of burning laces the air and I feel it in the back of my throat, know too that it is something that will lodge in my memory. I have stayed longer than I wanted and with each step I start to plan the details of my return journey, try to find some respite from the heat wavering the horizon by thinking of the sea. Of walking on the beach. Of Hannah sitting in the kitchen of my house sometime in the future and, in a welcome reversal of roles, me making her coffee. I try to construct these images as a way of creating a conduit back into the world I have left, a world which, however increasingly lonely I felt, appeared at least to offer the security of the familiar. Of things being in some kind of order where, even if they slipped, it would be the result of my own actions and not through some dangerous and unpredictable sequence of events over which I had no control, something that now seems an inevitable result of entering Donovan's orbit once more.

We go inside and he produces cold drinks out of a fridge that seems to spend its whole day whining about the strain of keeping its motor running. Melissa excuses herself, obviously upset. Donovan stands at the window staring out and it is as if the incoming light streams through his frailty. I know that after I leave I will never see either of them again. That it is almost time for me to go.

'What is it with the poles, the totem-like poles?' I ask.

'They're not totem poles,' he says, turning to face me. 'They're something you can understand if you'll let yourself. They point the way but they're more than that. So much more. We all need to lift up our eyes from this world, need to look up. And not just with our eyes, Mikey, not just with our eyes. You know the story in the Bible when the children of Israel are in the desert and they get bitten by snakes? And Moses raises up a brass serpent on a pole and anyone who looks up at it in faith is healed, even those with the poison coursing through their body.'

He lifts his arm as if to point to a brass serpent and the light shoots through his spindle thinness.

'But you have to believe, Mikey, you have to believe to be cured. That's what we're doing here in this wilderness, turning our backs on temptation and making something that the suffering can look up at, find the help they need.'

He steps forward a few paces from the window and more light sidles into the room, making a fine filament of dust tremble about him. The same way it did all those years ago when I was boy choosing my books in a small-town library, a place in which I was offered another way and first experienced what I thought was love.

'You remember your Bible stories, don't you?'

'Sure,' I say, 'they were the first stories I ever heard,' but I don't tell him that only one still dwells deeply fixed in my consciousness, unable to be shaken free.

'It's what I had to do. Turn my eyes in a different direction. Look up. Make things with my hands. Honour the earth. Believe that the next hungry, sun-blistered soul stumbling through here might be the angel.'

He rubs his eyes, and I'm not sure whether it's to see more clearly or because tears are starting, but the idea of Donovan crying is something more than I can bear and I turn my head away until he composes himself once more. Then, in what suddenly feels like my final chance, I take advantage of this second moment of unexpected vulnerability to seize the opportunity.

'What happened to Tuyen, what happened to her child?'

'Mikey, Mikey,' he says, turning again to the window.

He stares out and a silence settles on the room.

'I need to know, Iggy. I just need to know.'

'I know that, Mikey,' he says, without turning around. 'You always need to know. Always needed to know you were doing the right thing, even when, because of where we were and the times we found ourselves in, doing the right thing wasn't always possible any more. And you, as much as anyone, know I didn't understand what the right thing was. I was lost, Mikey, trapped inside my own darkness, unable to lift my eyes to something better.'

'So what happened to her?' I persist, desperate to cut through this psychobabble.

'There was confusion everywhere,' he says, slowly facing me, holding both his hands palms upwards so that dust seems to drift through the splay of his fingers. 'Everything was falling apart. Everyone was getting out and those who couldn't get out were going into hiding. She got away — that's all I know.'

But I don't believe him and he sees the disbelief in my face.

'My memory's not good, Mikey. Things get jumbled up. Faces and names don't always match up any more. Once I could list the winners of the World Series in sequence — right back to Boston Americans, all the way back. Now I don't know what I did yesterday.'

'Tell me, Iggy. Did you try to get her out? Tell me the truth,' I say, angry that when it came to the crunch he sought refuge in a weakness that the rest of his life would have disdained.

'That's enough, Mikey,' Melissa says, suddenly appearing from the kitchen.

Donovan drops his hands to his sides and shakes his head slowly like a punch-drunk boxer waiting for the towel to be flung in the ring. But I have used up my compassion. Melissa comes and stands beside Donovan, resting a hand on his shoulder, and I wonder what her touch feels in the ebb of his physical strength. Does it merely serve to strengthen her love or does the emptiness fill her with fear?

I know about fear — all my life it has been a silent companion, always suppressed and always hidden but lurking in the shadows, glimpsed over the shoulder like a secret follower. Was it the curse of the firstborn? It feels sometimes like the greatest failure of my life and one that I would have given anything to discard. And as Melissa stands with her hand on Donovan's shoulder I remember the tightness of the embrace in which my mother and father held us as we hid in the basement, an embrace that was unable to stop what passed over and through me. But I think too of the night I stood with Julia amongst a people and shared their belief that they were at the door of a future determined by hope. And it was hope I wanted, believed it was hope that would save us.

I go to speak but Melissa's voice rings out, telling me again to leave it, and I wonder how much she knows about what happened in his past. But there is no way to sidestep her protection and it feels as if Donovan has once more evaded the things for which he was responsible. So as my resentment bridles I tell them I am leaving and start to make my way to my room to collect my stuff.

'We need you, Mikey,' Donovan says, and his voice is stronger.

'Need me?'

'Yes, Mikey, we need you. There isn't anyone else. No one else we trust.'

I am confused. He invites me to sit and reluctantly on my part we resume the seats we occupied the night before. There is something uncharacteristically nervous in his manner and, although we are inside, the sweat spots on his shirt have increased in number and size. He asks me if I want a drink but I say no, keen that nothing should delay my departure longer than is necessary.

'What is it you need?'

'I know I've asked you to do things in the past that troubled you. And you were right to be troubled. So asking now again after all these years doesn't come easy. If there was any other way, I wouldn't ask.'

'What is it you want, Iggy?'

'I want you to leave here, leave very soon. But with a passenger.'

'A passenger?'

'Yes, someone who needs to go north,' he says, hesitating. 'You're the only person who can take him.'

'And who is this passenger?'

He stands up and pulls the front of his shirt free from his skin then stares at the blackened remnants of the fire before turning to me again.

'You remember Corley Rodgers – Corley, Corley, Tell a Story Rodgers? We used to laugh at him. Well no one's laughing now because Corley finally found himself a story. He turned up here making a film about the border and, for better or worse, our paths crossed. He made his film and I thought that was that. But he came back, Mikey, and he brought someone with him. Someone who's been hiding out here ever since.'

I start to understand. Understand what is going to be asked of me.

'It's a guy who knows things – and it's better you don't even have his name or he yours. He knows bad stuff, Mikey, really bad stuff. And the country needs to hear what he has to say, needs to know what's being done in our name. They're looking for him – he can't stay here much longer. He's going north and on again – you don't need to know where. All you have to do is drive him to a place where others will pick him up and take him onwards. A day's drive – that's all.'

In all the times Donovan had asked me to do things the voice he used had commanded and been marked by a latent aggression. Now I hear none of that. And if he told me he needed me to stand up straight and true I would hightail it out that door, but he hasn't and when he speaks again it is to plead. I would be doing a good thing, a right thing, and he believes I will do it because that is the person I am. A better person than any of them. He makes it sound as if I am going to ring the Liberty Bell. And when I tell him I'm not prepared to be an accessory to a crime, and a serious crime at that, he tells me that I have no knowledge a crime has been committed. None of them have. That nothing has been made known to me or shared with me. And it will stay that way.

I need to try and explain what happens next, but it still doesn't make full sense to me and it always comes out differently so I'm not sure what is afterthought and what passed through my mind at the time. It isn't anything to do with Donovan any more because I finally know I don't need his approval or carry any obligation to him and I tell myself that, setting aside some shameful private moments that are sadly part of any human life, I've observed the accepted rules of whatever game I found myself playing. Observed them pretty strictly. The fears I have now about where my country is heading had not then grown into what they were soon to become. So why, then, do I find myself even considering Donovan's request? A request that goes against every concept of service I have ever harboured, an action tainted by the word 'treason' – one of those seemingly antiquated words but whose intimidating weight reaches into the modern world – and not just to my country but to the very ideals I thought my life had been built upon. I don't know but just maybe a lifetime of service allows you a sense of your debt being paid, of entitling you to a new freedom of thought and action once that indentured service comes to an end. I truly don't know, even though a day rarely passes without me trying to unravel its mystery and construct different paths that I might have followed.

'He's in the barn, Mikey,' Donovan says. 'He's a good kid. Pretty scared, as he should be.'

'I can't do this,' I tell him.

'We need you, Mikey,' Melissa says. 'He has to be moved on.'

'Otherwise it's just a matter of time,' Donovan adds.

I shake my head. This has nothing to do with me and to get involved in it is both dangerous to me in the present and to the reputation I have spent a lifetime securing. It's a non-starter, a violation of every value my whole career instilled in me. But slowly other things, only partially repressed, come into play and not least the simple fact that life itself doesn't always observe the rules by which you'd like your existence to be governed. So it took my wife at the very moment when we were supposed to share our lives most closely and steeped my remaining days in loneliness. It broke all the promises that we once made to those who helped us and who we left behind. It took my father's lifelong strength and singularity of vision – his rock of ages – and robbed him of himself. And so slowly a seed of doubt is sown and I start to wonder what my existence would be if even once I stepped outside the confines of a life I had predestined by making it subservient to a particular code and an unbending and fixed set of contexts that, if I'm honest, were sometimes at variance with who I really am. Wonder whether I could live a life untainted by fear. In those confused moments, with Donovan and Melissa looking at me, I think too of the old man, his whole life given to struggle and consumed by weariness, who remembers seeing lions come down to the beach at dusk and how that memory sustains him. But though I search I can't find a guiding image to hold fast to in the moment when I need it most, and that feels like an irreversible loss.

As I stand under the intense scrutiny of Donovan and Melissa, I feel suddenly at the very edge of worlds, with both the hope and danger that this brings; I see too the young man we interrogated in the prison, the photograph of his family who probably never saw him again. I remember the way he looked at me out of the bruised and discoloured flesh of his face. And then I think about who is hiding in the barn, a man unclothed who knows too much and who will come to understand the danger that knowledge brings. The knowledge of good and evil. I almost envy him that certainty, that unclouded and untrammelled clarity. But not what is waiting for him down the line. I know we don't forgive such as him. But for a few seconds it feels as if it is my soul that is still in limbo, and my voice one of those that Donovan heard on the wires, and when eventually I speak it sounds strangely ethereal, travelling far from myself into an unfathomable distance.

'I'll take him,' I say.

They both look at each other and I see their surprise. Melissa comes and hugs me and I feel the silver shock of her hair brush the side of my face.

'You're a good man, Mikey. A good man,' she says.

'All you're doing is giving a guy a ride,' Donovan says. 'That's all you ever need to say. You don't know who he is or anything about him. Soon others will take him off your hands, do what needs to be done.'

I don't say anything, not because I am already thinking of changing my mind but because there is one last opportunity and if it looks like a pay-off I don't care. Melissa goes to get my passenger ready and Donovan hurries into the kitchen, returning a few minutes later to hand me a wad of money and an address.

'If you need to pay for anything use this, not cards, and don't use your phone,' he says. 'Don't stop unless you have to and then make it as short as possible.'

'I'll take him if you tell me what happened to Tuyen.'

He looks shocked but then forces a half-smile as he says, 'You've learned important stuff – always negotiate from a position of strength. That's right, Mikey.'

He nods slowly as if in some reluctant show of admiration. I say nothing, knowing that for better or worse I have played my strongest hand.

'Why were you in La Porte Bleue that day?' he asks.

'Quyen came to me the night before and asked me to marry Tuyen, said it was the only way to get her out. That you weren't going to help them because she was pregnant with your child.'

'It's not true that I wasn't going to help her get out. I know why they'd think that, but it wasn't true, and I'd come that same day as you to tell them that I'd finally got seats on a plane. Pulled every string I could, traded in every favour ever owed me. But we were both too late, Mikey. They'd gone, disappeared into the chaos, and there wasn't any way of finding them. All the networks just vanished like snow off a ditch. People cut and ran if they couldn't get a seat out. Every one of them had no other impulse in their head but to disappear, to make a home run to wherever in the world kept them safe. To do whatever they needed to survive. They'd heard what had happened in Hue and fear multiplied by the hour. By the minute. There was not much more left than the bunch of Marines in the Embassy, not a single line I could follow or call I could make. I tried, Mikey, I really tried.'

'So what do you think happened to her?'

'She might have got out. Vien knew a lot of people from way back. He knew the French. He had contacts.'

'And if they didn't?'

'At best a re-education camp. The worst I don't want to think about.'

He sits down as if the strain of remembering has exhausted him.

'It's all I know, Mikey, all I know.'

I say nothing and try not to think about the worst. And then when I look at Donovan I see in this moment of surrender to his own frailty the cold wind that is coming steadily towards him, blowing through his existence on the earth, turning every atom that once formed who he was into dust. And there is an inescapable sadness about that, as there is about any human loss.

Melissa reappears and with her stands a young man, dark-haired, slender, wearing a plain blue cotton shirt with sunglasses clipped into the breast pocket, jeans and Converse. Over one shoulder is slung a sports bag so he looks as if he is just on the way to the gym. He comes towards me with an outstretched hand and calls me sir, thanks me. No names are exchanged – he is evidently well-versed in the etiquette of the situation.

'You're welcome,' I say, reciprocating the conventions of good manners while simultaneously wondering if this is the person who will start my life down unexpected paths.

I have committed, however, to a course of action and, for better or worse, I won't go back on it. But there is something I have to be sure of, so I look him in the eye, struck once more by his youthfulness and a kind of fresh-faced innocence – or is it naivety? – as if the world has not yet left its stain, and ask, 'Are you sure?'

'I'm sure,' he answers and then there is nothing more to be said except to take my leave.

Melissa hugs me for the second time and I let my hand rest on the coarse splayed swathe of her hair before she kisses me on the cheek and steps away. Donovan eases himself out of his chair and comes slowly towards me. He holds out his hand and just for a second I hesitate, then shake it.

'You're a good man. A good man,' he says.

'I try,' I say. 'We all try.' But it sounds hopelessly feeble, not even close to what I want my final words to him to be.

We head out to the SUV and stow our bags in the back. I don't direct him but my passenger opens the rear door and lies down in the space behind the front seats. It is obviously his accustomed position. I say nothing, lower my window and look for the last time at Donovan and Melissa as they stand shoulder to shoulder on the veranda, then spray water on the windshield to try and clean the stipple of dead insects and dust spots. Donovan raises his skinny arm in farewell but no further words are spoken and I set off, glancing finally at one of the poles they have erected, see how the light seems drawn to it and plays in the mosaic of blue tiles and the white bleached bones.

Apart from my occasional enquiry as to whether my passenger is OK, we hardly speak at all. Then an hour or so in I hear him say, 'I'm grateful.'

'Just giving a guy a ride back to the world,' I answer.

'Sure,' he says and then, after a pause, 'Iggy says you served with him in Nam.'

'The only word wrong in that sentence is "with".'

'He says you were one of the last ones out,' and he sounds just like the young men who mistook me for something other than a REMF.

'Only because I was so unimportant that they almost forgot about me. Iggy's memory isn't so good any more.'

'Anyway,' he says, 'I appreciate this.'

Then I remember something I have tried all my life to forget.

'There's nothing I need to say to you because you will take your own path now, except this one thing. If you have a photograph of anyone you love in your wallet or in your bag, you should think about taking one last look at it and then destroy it.'

'Why?'

'Because they will use it to hurt you. Because it makes you vulnerable.'

Silence settles again as we head north, driving past towns and cities whose names speak of the shared configuration of history, of saints and angels, of battles fought and land defended. In time we will hear talk of building higher and stronger walls but still they'll come. And maybe Donovan is right and the whole world is crossing over. Now I find myself a ferryman. And yes, there are times as I drive that I think what I should do is deposit him in the hands of his pursuers, receive the commendation of the state I had served all my life. At a gas station I have to stop and refill. He slips out and goes inside to use the restroom. I watch him walk across the forecourt, the back of his shirt heavily creased, but a young man seemingly without a care in the world. The automatic doors wheeze open as he approaches before he disappears inside, hidden behind the sun's glare on the glass. When he returns he hands me a drink and, as I cup the welcome coldness of the can, I'm glad he wasn't privy to my thoughts in those few minutes when he was out of sight.

Once, outside a small town, we come upon an accident involving a truck and a motorhome, with a police car, its lights flashing, parked up at the side of the road and a police officer ahead waving on the slow-moving line of traffic. We are waiting in line, slowly edging forward then stopping again when traffic heads in the other direction, given right of way. I tell him to stay low. The car in front has a Confederate flag on its fender and one that says 'Live Free or Die'. Soon there will be other stickers talking of making America great again and they will give their votes to the man they believe able to do it, just as my home town on the prairie will also believe – something that will leave me feeling homeless, a refugee in my own country, separated from the very people who guided me into the world and nurtured me as a child of the nation.

From a car two up, with its windows down, comes the sound of loud rap music and I can see heavily ringed fingers beating a rhythm on the outside of the driver's door. We edge forward a few more yards. Close to the motorhome a young family huddle at the side of the road while an officer with an open notebook takes a statement. It doesn't look as if anyone has been seriously hurt but parts of both vehicles litter the edges of the highway, the debris of bruised and twisted chrome hastily kicked to the side where light fastens and feeds on it.

We move again. This is the point of no return. We have almost drawn level with the officer directing traffic. Shades hide his eyes and, despite the heat, his crisply pressed uniform makes it look as if he has just come on duty. There is a broad wedding ring on the hand he uses to beckon us forward. Ten spies were bad, two were good. A small boy singing a chorus on a wooden pew, doing the actions with his hands. Were the ten spies bad because they couldn't see the goodness in the Promised Land revealed to them? But did the two supposedly good tell all of the truth? I can't be sure any more. Can't be sure in those seconds, as we draw ever closer, who is in the back of the SUV I am driving. All it would take is for me to wind down the window. But I drive slowly on with a friendly wave of my hand and, strange as it is, in that very moment I begin to feel a lightness in what I am doing, rather than a weight, almost as if I am unburdening myself of something and yes, just maybe, this is my own act of atonement.

I am already disorientated, disconnected from the things I believe are the ballast in my life, but in some unfamiliar way I have started to think of them as cargo, cargo that has broken loose and that, when the storm hits, might be jettisoned. Jettisoned to help you stay afloat in swirling and dangerous seas. Abandoned to help you reach the safety of shore and that in life instinct might be as good a guide as any. And yes, during the long hours of that journey in my mind my silent companion becomes my secret sharer who at a particular location and at a particular time will slip 'into the water to take his punishment: a free man, a proud swimmer striking out for a new destiny'. After I pass him over in the parking lot of a run-down mall he shakes my hand and I wish him luck but I never see him again except a year later on the front pages of newspapers and on my television. And whatever romance Conrad's words have engendered in my head is dispelled in time by the weight of his fate, his solitary confinement and vilification in the columns of those national papers owned by vested interests. My name comes into public proximity with his only once, when I sign a petition calling for his release from solitary and a review of his sentence. That of course is going to change if I ever let this story find a place in the world. But I care about other things now.

I understand, too, why Donovan set up the poles and, despite everything I know about him in the past we shared, it seems to possess its own beauty, to make something human in the wilderness, the wilderness that has always stood at the edge of our history. The wilderness where, as he said, all of us must come at some moment in our lives to face our own tests. But beauty remains in the eye of the beholder and in time we will have a president who thinks barbed wire can also be a beautiful sight. I know which I prefer. So I drive on across the invisible ley lines of history where countless journeys have been made, and not just in one direction. As a nation we have always been a people making new frontiers, pushing ever further into what lies beyond – it's the spirit that exists at the heart of who we are – even though when George W. Bush, in his attempt to launch a global war on terrorism, talked of 'extending the frontiers of freedom', he ended up working off the wrong map, drawing a line in the wrong sand. And there's still a price to be paid for that in what we did to others and what we did to our own.

In a different story, one that's fictional, at this point the narrative would probably head in a new direction, play itself out to a predetermined ending, planned out right from the first word written. I'd tell you about escapes, about small boats setting out at night and subject to storms and attacks from pirates. I'd describe the dark, all their hopes and churning fears. Selfishness and altruism. Tell you about dramatic rescues from sinking craft and despairing stasis in refugee camps. Describe endless searches on my part, frustrating dead-ends, the piecing together of clues from dusty official ledgers and eyewitnesses and then, like one of those long-lost-family-reunited television programmes, and to the literary equivalent of appropriate heart-tugging music, end with an encounter. A nervous encounter between a man and woman grown old, and her adult child, that slowly blossoms into love. Something that gives our hearts the comfort, the needy reassurance we desire more and more in the face of this fragmenting world. But if that's what you want, you need to look elsewhere because it's not something I'm able to give you.

So far I have told you only what I believe to be true, and that compulsion endures more than ever now, and so it behoves me to tell you that, as I drove north to that rendezvous in the parking lot of a dying shopping mall, I finally let Tuyen and her unborn child go, let them also slip into the dark and hidden waters of history. If I had retained the religious faith of my childhood, I would have said a prayer for them and their crossing over, but as that was long gone all I could do was look out at the landscape we were journeying through and in the ochre-coloured stretch of scrubland, or in the sky, try to find something to which I might lift my eyes. I told myself that after all these years maybe I too had crossed over, from that young man in his first day in Saigon when, despite the heat and dressed in my well-worn jacket, I headed off to start a lifelong career as a

REMF. It is late in the day to become a soldier and perhaps even a little duplicitous to try and assume a bravery never really felt. But sometimes you just step through an open doorway, step through it for better or worse.

After my passenger has departed – the exchange completed in under a minute in an almost empty parking lot – I drive on in silence, the featureless repetition of the landscape unravelling before me as I follow the highways that will bring me back to more familiar worlds and a flight home. Then comes the old familiar press of fear. My childhood nightmare restored unchanged to the present. Have we painted our lintels with blood? Will the terrible plagues and the dark angel sweeping in from the desert pass over us? I want to believe, have to believe that, despite everything that has happened, and in the absence of any other sustaining faith, love will keep me safe if only I can find it once more, and even if it sounds hopelessly naive, that despite every turning gyre of our history it is what we need to have on the nation's lintels.

I think again of Donovan, and his moment of leaving beneath a panoply of watching stars, and somehow I too am there as the pyre is lit, standing in the sudden shudder of flames as he sets out on his final crossing. And as my hands grip the wheel, with the heat-buckled road wavering like a mirage in front of me, I hear myself say aloud, 'Ashes to ashes. Dust to dust.' Then the unrelenting highway fades into the distance and I see instead the churning funnel of smoke slowly blending into the dark cloister of the night, until eventually they become one indivisible thing, the wind scattering him to the elements as he crosses over, under the same unblinking stars that look down on all our end.

ACKNOWLEDGEMENTS

In the writing of this book I was indebted to many sources, but in particular to Frank Snepp's *Decent Interval*, his magisterial and insider account of America's departure from Vietnam.

I am also indebted, as always, to Alexandra Pringle, Sarah-Jane Forder and Allegra Le Fanu.

A NOTE ON THE AUTHOR

David Park has written ten novels and two collections of short stories. His novel *Travelling in a Strange Land* won the Kerry Group Irish Novel of the Year. He has won the Authors' Club First Novel Award, the Bass Ireland Arts Award for Literature, the Ewart-Biggs Memorial Prize and the American Ireland Fund Literary Award. He has received a Major Individual Artist Award from the Arts Council of Northern Ireland and been shortlisted for the Irish Novel of the Year Award four times.

A NOTE ON THE TYPE

The text of this book is set in Perpetua. This typeface is an adaptation of a style of letter that had been popularised for monumental work in stone by Eric Gill. Large scale drawings by Gill were given to Charles Malin, a Parisian punch-cutter, and his hand-cut punches were the basis for the font issued by Monotype. First used in a private translation called 'The Passion of Perpetua and Felicity', the italic was originally called Felicity.